CAROLE MALLORY

POSEIDON PRESS

NEW YORK
LONDON
TORONTO
SYDNEY
TOKYO

Copyright © 1988 by Carole Mallory
All rights reserved
including the right of reproduction
in whole or in part in any form.
Published by Poseidon Press
A Division of Simon & Schuster Inc.
Simon & Schuster Building
Rockefeller Center
1230 Avenue of the Americas
New York, NY 10020
POSEIDON PRESS is a registered trademark of Simon & Schuster, Inc.
Designed by Karolina Harris
Manufactured in the United States of America
10 9 8 7 6 5 4 3 2 1
Library of Congress Cataloging-in-Publication Data
Mallory, Carole.
    Flash.

    I. Title.
PS3563.A43159F55   1988   813'.54   88-4181
ISBN 0-671-64464-5

an acknowledgment

to: Walter Anderson, Margaret Atwood, Sean M. Burns, Steve Cannon, Dr. Patrick Carnes, Ian Dove, Lita Eliscu Dove, Jane Gelfman, Betty Ann Grund, Michael Lally, Heather MacRae, Ann Patty, Mary Reinhart, Francesco Scavullo, Paul Wasserman, Irene Webb, Chester Wilson and H.P.

FOR MY MOTHER

7

WHENEVER I touch cold tile, I remember praying for a bathroom lock.

"Privacy. Who wants privacy?" Mom would shout through the door just before barging in. She would hold that worn rubber bag as if it were the Topkapi diamond. "This won't take a second. Get down on your knees and relax. You know you always feel better when it's over."

Then she would work that nozzle in, and did it hurt! That never stopped Mom. She kept shoving. Soon enough it did fit. Mom knew what was best. You bet.

That was then. Tricycle time on Easterly Road, Allentown, Pa. My childhood. Now she's learned to leave me alone. A little.

As I return to the bedroom for a suitcase, my past comes back to me. But then it's all up on the walls and all over my mother's apartment. Paintings from U. of P.'s art classes and covers from modeling days hang under fluorescent lighting in metal frames from Lamston's in the Lehigh Valley mall. (Mom's a mall groupie.)

When I did the *Time* cover, Mom thought my red hot pants were too short. For *Esquire* the "Pet Me I'll Purr" T-shirt was too tight. In *Elle* my bikini was too small, and in *Vogue* my neckline too revealing. She approved of the covers I did for *Mothers-to-Be* and *McCall's*.

My father liked them all. He liked anything I wore, anything

I did. His sole disappointment was that I was never on the cover of *U.S. News & World Report.*

As I fasten the buttons of my silk shirt, I fondle my breasts. They haven't changed since the days I modeled. Modeling bras for ads paid big bucks. Top manufacturers wanted my pert breasts. I never wanted their bras. My face and voice were bankable too. I still live off the money my body has earned. Just a month ago a former client asked me to be photographed in a bikini for a poster promoting his latest line of swimwear. I gave an autographed copy to Mom at Christmas. She cut off my bikini-clad body and pasted my severed, still-smiling head in her scrapbook. I was not surprised.

Grabbing an antique silver necklace and wrapping it around my neck, I return to the bathroom and adjust each strand.

"Maya, what are you doing in there?"

I thrust my chest out and stand erect, just as I did before the camera.

"You'll miss your train if you don't hurry up."

Playing with the chains makes time stop.

Mother's footsteps. Now she barges into the bathroom, wearing a polyester pantsuit. She never wears skirts.

"My goodness, child, you can see right through your blouse."

My shoulders droop.

"Aren't you ashamed to dress that way?"

I try not to listen, and return to the bedroom.

"Put a jacket over yourself!"

I slip on a blazer.

Sometimes I think my mother's perverse. Then again, maybe she's just being Pennsylvania Dutch. Being the eldest in a family of fourteen with a handicapped father and an alcoholic mother had made her feel like the man in the family. When I wasn't angry with Mom, I felt sorry for her and would do anything to make her happy, almost anything.

"Be good," she says, "and stay away from those sex-starved men. Keep that jacket on!"

"Mom, that's enough!" I close my suitcase and carry it to the living room filled with unmatched pieces of overstuffed furniture, a twelve-inch TV, African violets, a small aluminum Christmas tree and a caged parakeet.

"Why don't you get a nine-to-five job?"

"Didn't I just wish you Happy Birthday? I take that back." The parakeet squawks.

"Birthdays don't mean a thing to me. Who wants to be seventy-four?" Mom goes into the kitchen and brings back a shopping bag filled with goodies.

I get my ten-year-old mink out of the closet and drop it on the plastic-covered Barcalounger. "Well, I won't come home next year, if you keep this up. I'll love you courtesy of Pacific Telephone."

We hug and kiss. My mom, Elsie Mae Dunkelburger (why I changed my name to Endicott), smiles, revealing her one dimple. "I love you, Maya, you know I do." I smell freshly baked shoofly pie.

Releasing her four-foot-eleven bundle of willpower, my five-foot-six pillar of anxiety is out the door—suitcase, mink, shoofly pie and all. I run down the hallway past senior citizens looking for action. Back to the real world.

A stocky driver stands by a Red and White cab. His chubby hand reaches for my suitcase and throws it into the trunk. I open the back door and slide in.

Accidentally, I swear it! my wraparound skirt opens to the center of my pink satin bikinis. The driver gets in, looks back, pauses.

Something goes off inside me. Call it a buzz. Call it a hum. It's real. I close the door, and my body tingles. I read his name on the taxi license over the glove compartment.

Raphael Garcia Llopis drives off. I like Mexicans. Black eyes. Black eyebrows, bushy and overgrown. Black hair full of hair cream. His lower lip protrudes, exposing the inner pink lip. His upper lip is hidden by a moustache. Dark curls run down his

neck, disappear under his green baseball jacket, pop up on the
back of his hands. His fingernails are dirty.

No scratched plastic partition comes between us. In the rearview mirror I study his eyes. He watches me, then the road,
then me.

I feel flashes. (Here we go again.)

Where are my sunglasses? They make me feel safe. I hunt
down my Ray-Bans in the caverns of my pocketbook and put
them on. It begins to rain. He looks nervous.

He has one of those stupid faces that love sex. He is not into
becoming rich or famous. Good old working class. Loves to
fuck. Poor idiot. He's as bored with driving his lousy cab as I
am close to crazy after three days in my mother's house. Every
day the same nine-to-five drudgery. He's given up the fight. His
spirit is sucked; he's a follower. Give him a road and a passenger,
and off he goes. Whoopee! Schmuck.

I feel sorry for the poor asshole. Better believe it. My legs
open wider. His eyes continue to look at me in the rearview
mirror. We stop at a red light.

He turns around, showing a mouth of gold crowns. "Would
you like some music?"

"Sure." Why not? I smile as if I don't know what's going on
either. I can't think.

"Nice view, lady."

"Think so?"

Who's he kidding? I pull my legs up to my chest. My skirt
falls away to both sides.

"Hey, we're about to go on the highway," he says. He can't
think either.

"So?" Just as the traffic next to us starts up, I pull off my
panties and draw my spread legs back up to my chest.

"Jesus Christ!"

He thinks. He recovers. "Maybe," he says, "you want to get
off at an exit and have me join ya?"

Silence.

"Huh?"

"Drive!"

As we round the bend entering the highway, my chains brush against my breasts. The nipples are standing up like maraschino cherries. My right hand plays with them; my left does things with my skirt.

"Sex-o-matic. Sex-o-MA-tic," Prince screams over WIBG.

Breathing deeply, I squeeze my buttocks to the beat.

Now my right hand undoes the buttons on my shirt. Oh, Mom, if you could see me now. I keep looking at Raphael Garcia Llopis, right in his rearview. I rub each chain over each nipple. My head arches. Poor guy. He is looking back every chance he can. Traffic whizzes by us.

He turns his head for an instant, 180 degrees, like a devil. We're going 60 mph. I spread my knees more and move to the beat. My beige knee socks are still on, and my shirt is open all the way. That's what I used to be. An ad. I sold sex. Look at me, but don't touch me. You can't.

"Lady, I've got to slow down if you keep this up." He looks back again. He wets his lips. It is a funny chewing gesture, almost grotesque.

I like it. It's very Latin. He's weird. Stupid. I rub on. What do I care about him? Or cars going by? I'm hot. Hot all over. Like I rarely am. Never argue with what makes you hot. Laying my head back on the seat, I stroke the hood. Tip of my pleasure. Trees blur. Billboards pass. Gardner's Gin. That was me once, smiling under an umbrella, selling gin. You drank Gardner's and you got someone like me. Lucky you! I was on the buses and trolleys of the Northeast corridor for three full years.

"Look, lady, I got to pull off at the next exit."

"Shut up and drive."

He moans at the sight of my secrets. "We're gonna have an accident," he says.

I push my pelvis upward into his gaze. I spread my legs on

his cracked maroon vinyl. I am about to burst. I let out a scream. It comes and comes and then it's over. My legs fold. I feel clean. Empty. Good.

"We're almost there. Want me to pull in an alley?" he asks.

"No." I pull my panties back on, fasten my skirt and shirt. I see Philadelphia's 30th Street Station ahead.

"Wanna get together later, lady?"

"Look, I've got a train to catch."

"I don't believe it! You do this all the time? I don't get it."

We stop in the loading zone.

I gather my handbag and overnight case and step from the cab. Mumbling to himself, he gets out and hands me my suitcase from the trunk. I give him the exact fare and walk off.

"Hey, lady, where's my tip?"

"Are you kiddin'? You had it, mister!"

Why do I do this every time I leave my mother's?

2

I run down the stairs for the Amtrak train to New York and board at Gate 11. Not only do I feel better, but I'm glad it's over. I collapse into the first free seat. What is it with me? Do other women ever do that? Men do, I know. But women?

Am I a pervert? Why cab drivers? And why must I get so angry? I couldn't do it if I didn't get angry. Orgasms aren't easy for me to come by. I'll do anything for that release. That's your daughter, Mom. An orgasm junkie. Well, chickadee, I tell her, flashing is safe. No evidence, no involvement.

I feel helpless. My mind won't quit. Where's the bar? Three cars ahead I buy a Bloody Mary and return with it to my seat of stained, faded black leather. Sitting on it feels rough, uncomfortable, but it beats being in that cab. Stale cigarette smoke bothers my sinuses. I watch the ice cubes in the cold plastic glass being jostled by the train.

Sometimes I feel there is a partition between the world and me, as if I'm merely looking at life, a permanent passenger. Mom told me I was born with a perfect body. If it's so perfect, why can't I enjoy it? Out the window, New Jersey is passing by. I remember how I felt when I first became pretty. I knew at once that being pretty plus good makeup added up to beauty. I learned to use it. I had to. My father suffered from a special deformity. He had had a lobotomy when I was thirteen, and his eyes no longer blinked. His nose ran. He drooled. He grunted.

His shoulders were hunched around his neck. He twitched violently. His smile was a pasty grin. People would stare and jeer.

Sometimes I could divert attention from him by looking my best. Then people would be more polite to Daddy. I resented the hypocrisy my appearance brought out in people. What if I looked just like him?

After he got sick, Daddy loved to read dirty books. He would hide torn-out pages under his mattress. Mom caught him once and hit him. He twitched away like a giant metronome. He stuttered forth a defense. I wanted to tell him to stash the pages in my shoe bags; she'd never look there.

Before the lobotomy he had been put in a psychiatric hospital in Philadelphia. No one knew what was wrong with him. The doctors thought it was mental. The nurses liked him, and said he ought to be out of the hospital. He helped them make beds. He made me ceramic ashtrays and a hooked rug. When he was released, the doctors told Mom he needed to have sex.

I don't think she took their advice. Soon he was back in the hospital. After the lobotomy—which he wanted—he was worse. He never made sense, and he was incontinent.

He never made sense? Did I?

"New York. Amtrak train from Philadelphia arriving in New York City."

I'm home. Well, I'm back in New York. Soon Hollywood is going to be home. My West Coast theatrical agent, Michael Stone, has asked me to move to L.A. "New York is OK if you wanna do stage," the Ivy League–looking Michael said, chuckling. "Personally I don't see that as your thing. Now if you wanna do movies or TV, you gotta move to Hollywood. Pilot season's coming up. You're a great type. Sexy women are in!"

The Michael Stone Agency—he's considered a young hotshot—is reputed to be one of the best on the West Coast. He doesn't have an East Coast office. As he said—or did he imply? —I'm not talented enough to do theater anyway.

I am happy to be wanted. There's nothing left for me in Manhattan, not after having been here for six years with one love, six
years now part of the past. My fiancé no longer wanted to marry
me, so I left him.

There is lightning, the crackling of thunder. It begins to rain
heavily. I grab a cab, as though nothing had ever happened to
me in a cab. We drive up Eighth Avenue, make a right and pass
Studio 54, the discothèque where I first met Jean-Paul. He had
blue eyes, brown shoulder-length hair and muscles that bulged
from under a faded rose-colored T-shirt and tight leather pants.
He was rather tall, very dark and extremely handsome. Just my
kinda guy. While my date was getting me a drink, I asked Jean-
Paul to dance. When the music ended, I had fallen in love. Then
he kissed my cheek. "Thanks," he said, "I needed that," and
returned to his wife, Sandy Katz, a short brunette from Bay
Ridge. A few months later they were divorced.

Jean-Paul told the lawyers he was destitute; he was.

One snowy night six months later I bumped into him in front
of Carnegie Hall. He was crying. One tear slid down his cheek.
I thought it was for me. Later I found out he had conjunctivitis.

He asked me to dinner the following evening. I made dinner.
I was dinner. He never left my apartment. He had no place to
go. He had only $300 to his name, and a twenty-year-old tennis
racquet (which accompanied him everywhere he went), yet he
had bought me a dozen white daisies. And though he was sad,
he made me laugh. His sense of humor wasn't funny, but ab-
surd—that delightful kind of Italian humor that can be corny
but oh-so-sweet.

When people asked him what it was like to be the son of
Alessandro, the famed Nobel Prize winner, Jean-Paul would
say, "Eh, eh, uh, uh," sticking out his tongue. "What's it like to
have a Jewish mother? What the fuck, everybody's got his problem." Then he would wave his hands and move like a clown, a
bit like Marcel Marceau, or was it Charlie Chaplin? He had
heart. Or so I wanted to believe.

I look at the cab driver. He is Greek, thin, dark-eyed, moustached. He belches. The taxi reeks of moussaka. We are passing the Plaza Hotel. Thunder. More rain.

I remember the first time I flashed—four months ago in Paris when I walked out on Jean-Paul. I checked into a small hotel, ordered room service and felt those tingling sensations begin. When the waiter entered, I did it. Then I feared I might be arrested, so I quickly put on a tweed suit and white silk shirt, and slicked my hair back into a bun. But nothing happened. My career as a flasher had begun.

My taxi has arrived at Sutton Place. Within seconds I'm at my apartment door, relieved that Philadelphia is behind me. I hate going home.

Tomorrow, Hollywood. In a few weeks I'll know if I got the part. I was tested three months ago. If Mother ever learned that I auditioned chained naked to a bed with a camera at my feet, she'd have a gallbladder attack. All the others had tested the same way. They told each of us we would have to do it if we wanted to get the starring role. And not only do I want the role, I want to be a star.

3

THREE months ago I agreed to audition for *The Starlet*. I had just flown out on Jean-Paul. We had been living between New York and Paris, where we stayed at his grandmother's carriage house on Avenue Foch.

One day in Paris I received a letter from my mother. It was in her frugal Pennsylvania Dutch style. It merely said that my father had attempted suicide. When I called home to Philadelphia, he was dead.

A year had passed since Jean-Paul proposed. It was apparent he was stalling. I was not going to return to Paris from my father's funeral without a wedding date.

"Do you still want to marry me?" I asked.

"I don't know," he said.

Was he too cowardly to tell me he had changed his mind? Or was he merely protecting his assets? Had he been advised by his lawyers how to handle me? Since his father's death a year before, Jean-Paul had become worth seventy million dollars.

Though I had left Jean-Paul hoping I would never want to see him again, I knew we would always be bound in a special way. We both had fathers who had been alive, but were no longer present for us.

Jean-Paul's father was world-famous, highly respected, incredibly wealthy; he had won the Nobel Prize for Literature. Jean-Paul's mother, Laurence, had never married his father,

Alessandro, though she gave birth to four of his children.

Fifteen years before Alessandro's death, Laurence walked out on the Nobel laureate, taking her four illegitimate children with her. Her two-month-old infant died on the journey to Paris from Alessandro's medieval castle, Palazzo della Vacca, outside of Rome. Jean-Paul and his sister continued to visit their father. But one year later when Jean-Paul attempted to see him, an angry Alessandro set dogs on his own son and tried to have him arrested. No one knew why. Some speculated. Laurence, Jean-Paul, his sister, Chanda, and his brother, Nicolas, never spoke to Alessandro again.

The wealthy Nobel laureate had left no will, so the government was about to dole out funds from his estate to Jean-Paul and his famous family. None of us could wait, but we had to.

Alessandro believed in immortality. "This made it impossible to relate to someone like me, who looks like him," Jean-Paul would say with a modest smile. The great Nobel Prize winner felt that drawing up a will would bring on death. And he despised Laurence, saying, "I can see her fighting to get to my estate, while I'll be looking down laughing." And fight she did. Years before his death she began a massive lawsuit against the Italian government.

After Laurence left, the Great Genius immediately married a plain, quiet artist with blond hair and blue eyes named Rosa. Laurence was far from plain, and quiet only when scheming.

Not long after Alessandro died, Laurence won her lawsuit against the Italian government. Jean-Paul was named executor of the will. No one else wanted the job. Rosa, who had no children, went insane and was committed. Jean-Paul's younger brother, Nicolas, at age fifteen had attempted to see Alessandro, and also met with rejection. Nicolas then tied himself to a tree in front of one of his father's villas, set himself on fire and died one month later. Chanda, the child who inherited the Great Genius's talent, didn't want to waste her time unraveling the governmental red tape. She wanted to pursue a career in interior decoration, have a glamorous social life and spend her money as soon as she could. But cleverly, like her mother, she did not let Jean-Paul know this. Instead she pretended she was helpless when it came to financial matters. (She was as helpless as a bomb over Pearl Harbor.) This falsely feminine stance, doubly false since Chanda was a dyke, appealed to Jean-Paul's lack of identity.

Now Jean-Paul delighted in his power to tell others what to do: lawyers who had mocked him, publishers who had ridiculed him, agents who had belittled him. No one would treat him like a bastard or call him one anymore.

I felt Jean-Paul was punishing me for what Alessandro had done to him, for my knowing the truth and for my having known him when he was destitute. With the Great Genius dead, and his new wealth and position, he thought he could buy a new identity. I had to be hidden along with the rest of the past.

We had been living on my savings for years. I couldn't accept being shut out of family matters, from Alessandro's newly discovered manuscripts and treasures, but most of all from Jean-Paul's feelings. He didn't want souvenirs from his scrounging past hanging around his life, and like a fool I played into his desires—I left him to attend my father's funeral, never to return. I left him voluntarily.

Before boarding the plane I asked him to return $5,000 he had borrowed. He went to the bank in the morning, met me at the airport, handed me the money and said with a pasty grin, "Here, shove it up your c-cunt."

For the entire eight hours on Air France I held Tutu, our French poodle, and cried and remembered I'd left behind the white silk shirt I'd bought on sale at St. Laurent for only $90. Who'd be wearing it now?

Tutu had been my salvation. When Jean-Paul shouted, threw things or took whacks at me, he barked. He pulled at his master's cuff like a miniature referee. After seeing the black temper of his owner, Monsieur Supertoots joined my side and became a feminist.

During the flight I thought that the one good thing about my father's death was that he wouldn't know Jean-Paul had jilted me. He had suffered enough. I thought back to the time of his lobotomy. I was a cheerleader at a pep rally. My mother didn't want him to have it; my father wanted it. He had just undergone seventeen shock treatments against his wishes. A neighbor had told Mom, "You should do something about Mr. Dunkelburger's twitching. Shock treatments helped the veterans of the Korean War." So Mom talked my father into having them. After each treatment he ran around the house like an animal on fire. He would lose his speech. Each morning over breakfast I taught him to speak again. After his series of shock treatments—now known to cause brain damage—my father was asked if he wanted a lobotomy. No wonder he said yes!

During the operation the doctors discovered he'd been suffering from Parkinson's disease, not a nervous breakdown. They apologized for their misdiagnosis, but Mother was still sent a bill for a thousand dollars.

"I told Daddy, 'Let those butchers try to collect.'" Mother would laugh, and Daddy laughed too.

I wore yellow to my father's funeral. My father wore the suit I'd had custom made for his deformed body. He had been planning to wear it to my wedding. Now he was out of his misery. That made me happy. But I wouldn't look at his waxlike, stuffed, made-up, reconstructed body in the coffin. Mom kissed him a lot. I sat on the far side of the room, sang along with the hymns and stared at the black box with one arm jutting out of it. He had such long slender fingers, like mine. I remembered cutting out my paper dolls by his feet when I was a little girl, while he worked at his general ledger. I'd felt safe. At peace. We had been a team—my father, the efficiency expert, and me. Not long after the operation with my tips from waitressing I paid for locks to be put on the inside of every door. Then he couldn't run away. He had tried.

When I returned to our penthouse in New York, I couldn't
leave the bedroom. With his new wealth Jean-Paul had wanted a
penthouse in New York and a huge flat in Paris. Only the
month before we had signed a three-year lease on the penthouse,
and as usual I had made the necessary payments with my savings. Who would be paying for it now?

My queen-sized hospital bed with its buttons and levers to
raise my feet—great for hangovers—seemed all too appro-
priate. I had bought it to live the luxurious life of my dreams, to
be chic, to act like a mad millionairess. That was my father's
dream. Napoleon Hill's *Think and Grow Rich* had been his bible.
He had been so proud of me for being engaged to the son of a
Nobel Prize winner.

4

DREAMS were over. Now nightmares began. Seconals and Valiums took me to sleep, along with wine. Days passed. The phone rang.

"It's Louise," a friendly, crackling voice said.

Silence.

"Your agent." Louise was a booker for my modeling agency, Click, and handled auditions for movies when the studios were looking for gorgeous model types. Louise was overweight, wore glasses, lived in New Jersey and was one of the kindest souls I had ever met. Unlike many bookers who were jealous and untrustworthy, Louise was always loving. She had known Jean-Paul. I was going to pay for her plane ticket to Paris for the wedding. Was.

I was still silent.

"Stop crying, girl. Please get your act together. I have an audition for you." Her voice was even more cheerful.

"How'd you know I was home?"

She didn't answer that. It didn't matter. "There's a film project," she said, "called *The Starlet*. It's based on the best-seller. The starring role has been offered to Cher, Jessica Lange and Darian Nelson. They all turned it down. None of these ladies will do the required nudity, so the studio's looking for a relative unknown, someone who's never had star billing. You'd be perfect. Interested?"

"Anything right now sounds good."

"Atta girl. Wear your sexiest outfit and go to 405 Fifth Avenue at eleven thirty tomorrow morning. Nick Elton is the casting director. I sent him your picture—the one of you in that crocheted job. Now he's eager to meet you. Forget your former freeloader. There are plenty of other abusive men out there." Louise laughed like a truck driver.

I cuddled Tutu, now without a father, and decided that for our survival, mistress and lapdog, I should go on the audition. I had to support him. He was worth every can of Ken-L-Ration (and more).

That night I swallowed my pre-audition preparation, Valium and wine. In the morning I pulled myself together with lots of coffee and danish. I craved sugar. It gave me a buzz.

I decided to wear a cobalt-blue suede dress with a ragged hem slashed in the front to show the inside of my thighs. With the suede dress, matching blue tights, lots of loose curls, blue eyes, crimson lips, blue suede boots, ivory bracelets that clattered when I moved my wrist. The look: Jane swinging out on Tarzan. The perfume: Jean Patou's Mille—a gift from Jean-Paul.

I walked into Nick Elton's office in the Zercon Films Building on Fifth Avenue. The blinds were half drawn, the windows New York dirty. A brass desk lamp illuminated my résumé and glossy photo neatly placed on a highly polished glass and mahogany desk. A big brown leather armchair was strategically placed so that whoever sat in it was visible, head to toe, to the person seated at the desk. Dog-eared copies of *Penthouse*, *Playboy*, *Vogue* and *Cosmopolitan* were stacked on a cocktail table in front of a well-worn brown leather sofa. Faded poster-size photos of Marilyn Monroe, Jayne Mansfield and Brigitte Bardot covered one wall. An empty coffeepot sat on top of a watercooler which appeared to be rarely used. Next to the watercooler was a small bar which appeared to be used frequently.

Nick Elton was post-preppy, prematurely graying, almost albino-looking. He stared at me through tortoiseshell glasses, arms crossed in front of his chest. He didn't move or speak. His eyes seemed to have neither lids nor life. Slowly he walked around me, taking in my body inch by inch. Thank God he didn't ask me to move. Most men who auditioned beautiful actresses and models got off on this. He glared as if he were judging a beauty contest.

As the silence intensified, my hands became cold, my muscles tense. My breathing was like a child's when hiding during hide-and-seek.

Whenever a casting director was this silent, he was flaunting his power, delighting in his manipulation. I had been through enough auditions to know not to begin the conversation; that showed fear.

Finally Nick Elton cleared his throat and said in a well-modulated voice, "So you're Maya Endicott. I like your photo very much. So does our director, Jacques René." Slowly he walked behind his desk, hips thrust forward, a peculiar rocking motion to his pelvis, and sat down.

I sat in the chair and crossed my legs without thinking. The deep slit in the front of my skirt opened wide. Quickly I placed my hands in my lap.

He studied my legs, particularly where they joined my hips. He held up the eight-by-ten glossy. A profile. My head and torso. I was inhaling deeply. Hands at play in windblown hair. Breasts pointing upward. Thighs spread. Back arched. Expression: "Go ahead. I'm ready." I loved the old photo. It had the courage I couldn't feel right now.

"Later in the week," Nick Elton said, "I'll arrange a meeting for you with the director. It is required you do some nudity." I noticed his eyes blink and blink again. "How do you feel about that?"

"No problem."

Jean-Paul had insisted I quit acting. He had a fear of what

actresses had to do. What I would do. I was ready to do anything, as my expression in the photo promised.

"Would you like some scotch? A director bought it to thank me for the casting I did on his film. Nice gesture, don't you agree?"

"Yes, but I think I'll take a rain check if you don't mind." Louise always warned me never to drink on an audition. Nick Elton's hands trembled as he held the scotch bottle. His eyes now blinked with every other sentence. His coming on to me was a drink away. Making a career out of auditioning for men— modeling—had made my instincts razor sharp. I had learned how to cock-tease when necessary, and how not to when absolutely necessary.

Seconds later I was out the door. Two days later I was back at the door, which this time was opened by a short, beady-eyed Frenchman, Mr. Jacques René. The director? The office looked like a pornographer's studio. Glossy photos of girls wearing bikinis and less were strewn across the desk, the cocktail table and all over the gold wall-to-wall carpet. Copies of *Penthouse* and *Playboy* were opened to centerfolds stained with coffee. Cigarette butts smeared with red and purple lipstick filled the ashtrays scattered about the room. The blinds were fully drawn.

Five big-breasted beauties in the shortest of skirts had been waiting in the outer office. One said, "Jackie René is a pig, a pussy lover who likes to pimp for studio heads." What did I care? I needed the job. I wanted to forget.

Mr. René looked like a pussy lover. He had whiskers, a small, thin, undernourished moustache, blotchy skin. He spoke ever so slowly. He pushed his Toulouse-Lautrec chin into the air, which made him appear to be looking down at me as I towered above him. Was this an indication of his directorial prowess?

"So you're Maya Endicott," he said in a nasal voice that, like his chin, had a condescending air. Power play. Auditions were nothing but power plays. This guy didn't care about talent. He felt superior to me because he thought he had something I didn't. The only thing he had that I didn't was his cock. Which he was undoubtedly thinking about what to do with as well. Shut up, I told myself. You need the job. Listen to the creep. I smiled as if I wouldn't know what a cock was.

Mr. René stood there waving my eight-by-ten glossy in the air. I looked down at him as though I were looking up to him— with admiration.

"I like this photo," he said as if he were holding an Oscar. "Very much. You do realize there is some nudity required on this film." (Here we go, I thought.) "I want to hear from you personally . . . right now . . . of any objections." Mr. René was breathing heavily. I was afraid to look at his crotch for fear he had an erection. His pants were so tight I knew it would show and then I'd have to react. I stayed glued to his eyes, muddy brown surrounded by yellow whites with red veins.

Act interested, I told myself. "I have no objection to nudity, Mr. René. But would you tell me a little about the character?"

He rolled his tongue over his lips and stuck both hands into his stretch jeans. "The heroine of *The Starlet* is a sex symbol. She has been kidnapped and held for ransom by: One, a truck driver. Two, a Vietnam war hero. Three, an ex-con. And four, an insurance salesman. These four have taken an oath not to touch our heroine." Mr. René was rocking back and forth on his feet while rubbing his hands, now deeply embedded in his pockets, up and down. "No complications. They agree. But she is so attractive that, one by one, they rape her." Suddenly Mr. René turned his back to me. His hands came out of his pockets. His buttocks were flat. No ass. (But an asshole.) His jeans were worn and stained. He thought he was hip. "She is forced to have sex with each one to survive." Slowly Mr. René pivoted on his heels and looked up at me, muddy-brown eyeball to cobalt-blue eyeball, tucked his Disneyland T-shirt tighter into his jeans and inhaled. "Eventually she murders one. Causes two of the others to kill each other. And falls in love with the fourth. Here's the scoop. Throughout the film she is chained to a bed. The first rape is what we'll shoot for the test. You will be asked to lie with your tummy on the bed." Mr. René stopped talking and took a deep breath as though he were entering the stage as Macbeth. "No frontal nudity." Mr. René bowed his head, looked at the floor, then paused.

I couldn't help thinking Mr. René would love playing the part.

The following week I was flown to Hollywood and placed in front of the cameras. They had added to the test. For the nude scene I was told I had to castrate one of the rapists with a .25 Beretta. I worked up tears for the job, keeping pictures of Jean-Paul and my father in my head. (I couldn't believe it, but when I came home I masturbated. The orgasm made me want to live.)

Mr. René smiled. "Miss Endicott, please drop your robe. Lie with your back on the bed. The crew will handcuff you to the headboard so we can set up the lights."

What back to the bed? I had been told *no frontal nudity!* I was willing to do anything but that.

I signaled to Mr. René. We must have a chat.

"Look, Miss Endicott, the other girls have done it. If you want to be considered, you must do what is required for the part. I don't make the rules for starring parts. The studio does."

I did as I was told. I wanted the part. Grips handcuffed my wrists to the headboard. Mr. René continued with the direction. "John James and Adam Cord will come in from either side of the bed and squeeze your tummy. Kick and lift your legs as if you were being raped. Don't forget, you are fighting for your life! All modesty must be abandoned. You must have no concern for what you look like. Only the desire to stay alive. Anything to stay alive. Disregard the camera." (It was at the foot of the bed.) "Concentrate on this feeling of being raped. As an actress, your body is your instrument. Use it! No one is trying to exploit you. We are merely trying to get the best film on you that we can. Studio executives must see that you can act.... MAKEUP!"

The makeup woman rubbed baby oil over me. The camera was focused. My breasts and hair were lit. I began to kick vigorously from side to side. I hoped I got that part. I wanted that part. Jean-Paul who?

5

THE day after the test I returned to New York to make my final move. I would leave my furniture and take to L.A. only my clothing and the bare essentials—Tutu.

I called Louise at Click to say goodbye.

"You sure you want to give up your clients and move to Tinseltown? Movies are cast on the East Coast. I don't care what that hotshot faggot agent of yours says."

"Louise, I need to get away."

"I understand. Just want you to know we love you, and you can always come back to Click. Heard your test was great. You're gonna get that part and be a big star. Don't forget the agency that discovered you!"

"I'll miss you, Louise. It feels good to have someone believe in me."

"Forget that Italian imposter. You'll find yourself a real prince like you deserve. Someone who loves you more than his tennis racquet. Kiss Tutu for me."

"You do it." I held the phone to his ear and heard Louise give him a big smackeroo.

Tutu licked the receiver. He had always liked Louise.

"Thanks, Louise. You're part of the family. Send you lots of postcards."

"You better." She laughed her caring laugh and hung up.

Within a week I had packed, dealt with movers, called Mom

to stay goodbye, closed up the penthouse and was on a plane to L.A.

A fast exit is the best exit.

For one week Tutu and I stayed at the Chateau Belmont on Sunset Boulevard. Daily he and I made the rounds to landlords in West Hollywood. Dogs were not permitted in most buildings. That didn't stop Tutu. By day five he had charmed the owner of a small cottage in Laurel Canyon that looked like a set from *Lost Horizon*. It had been Valentino's country home, built in 1929 by the architect who had designed Grauman's Chinese Theater, famous for its sidewalk with those footprints of the stars.

Tutu had found us a new home worthy of his paw prints. Once we moved in, I called an old friend from modeling days, Zoe Sargeant, red-headed, blue-eyed, beautiful—"Z" to her one hundred closest friends. All stars.

One summer this tall, flat-chested, big-buttocked beauty from Little Rock flew with me to Paris, where we were photographed for the couture collections by *Elle*. On the booking she complained, "Jean and Marie and I can only afford a studio apartment. One of us has to sleep out every night 'cause there's only two single beds. And Jean is a goddamn *virgin*. So she always stays home. Marie and I have to do all the work. Honey, I'm exhausted!"

Two weeks later Jean and I were on vacation in the South of France. Z refused to come to Saint-Tropez with us. She preferred Cannes and its Carlisle Hotel Terrace. There, each night she met a new group of Arabs who gave her gold presents and other goodies.

Back in New York that fall, toting our modeling portfolios, we bumped into each other on the 57th Street bus. A now more experienced Z lectured me: "A girl has to marry more than one rich man, Maya. Income tax takes half your alimony."

Today, however, Z is still on number one—Eric Sargeant, tall, blond, movie-star handsome, socially gracious and then some. Women want Eric. I'm an exception. He's too neat and wears too much hair cream for me. And his plucked eyebrows remind me of early modeling days I would just as soon forget. Dressed as a cabbie or covered in mud he might get mine up.

Eric is, more often than not, the unemployed king of the B films. His better source of income comes from being a celebrity at shoe conventions, going in for market scams and selling real estate to his friends, the stars.

Z was five months pregnant when she married Eric four years ago. Her marriage made all the newspapers, even the front page of the *National Enquirer*.

When the Mexican housekeeper is off, Chad, their three-year-old, is often locked in the bedroom with the TV. Z does not like baby-sitting.

Z and I had become close friends and confidantes, not because of the similarities in the men we both dated, but because of the similarities in the mothers we both had. Though I had never met her mom, I felt I knew her. She sounded like as much of a control freak as mine. A devout Mormon, she was against premarital sex and constantly condemned Z, who had to struggle for the right to lead a life different from the one imposed by Mom.

Thrilled that I had moved to L.A. and angry at the way Jean-Paul had treated me, Z wanted to find me a rich husband. She gave me lesson upon lesson about Hollywood, etiquette and men. Those bachelors she considered eligible she introduced to me. With each handshake I broke out in hives. But I was touched that she cared.

Despite hard-core materialism, Z has heart. And she is spiritual. Meditation precedes each party, audition (she's a starlet like me) or business deal. Each night she reads herself to sleep.

Harold Robbins is her god.

I'm three weeks in Hollywood, still up for that starring part, and Z is giving an "A" party. Luncheon at the Sargeants' seems like a good move for me. I grab my smallest black bikini, wrap a silk scarf around my hips and slip on spike-heeled wooden sandals to give my legs a Vargas Girl look.

I am out the door and in my red Fiat convertible. Top down in the middle of January. Unbelievable to a New Yorker. I speed along Sunset Boulevard while listening to a disco version of "There's No Business Like Show Business."

The Sargeants live in Bel Air—their fourth home in their four married years. Residences in this exclusive section adjacent to Beverly Hills are frequently hidden behind stone walls or tall, dense hedges, or are protected by wrought-iron gates with complicated electronic devices that monitor incoming guests.

The Sargeants' home sits open to the road. No gates. No buzzer system. It is a two-story, four-bedroom frame house with murky red shutters in need of a good coat of paint. The roof, partially covered in black plastic, is under repair; so is part of the house. A bulldozer is parked on the lawn.

I dodge ruts and a tricycle as I drive down the long, narrow, semicircular driveway, passing four Rollses, a Mercedes and a lemon Corniche, squeezing my Fiat in between a silver-gray Daimler and a black Porsche Targa.

A toy baseball bat and several wooden soldiers decorate the lawn. A cracked cement birdbath stands next to a trellis covered by magenta bougainvillea which frames the entranceway.

The door is ajar. I ring. and walk in. An ebullient Z waves from the opposite side of the living room. Her long red hair shines like an Irish setter's in the sun. Her tall, slim body is barely covered in a green polka-dot bikini that has only enough fabric for three dots and two tiny bows which tie on Z's not so tiny hips, her finest asset, especially when viewed posteriorly. Her teeth are Hollywood white, her nails teenage pink, her makeup nonexistent. Natural lip gloss covers her full smiling lips.

"Don't step on the carpet! Eric will have a shit fit!"

"Sorry, Z."

"Don't be. Just take off your shoes and put on these Peds." (By the door is a pile of socks with the Diedas label sewn on.) "We're trying to sell this joint. Hey, you're late. Why, girl?"

"Late night."

"Who?"

"Mick Hodges."

"God, where did you meet him?"

"At the Hollywood Hills Hotel pool." (My office . . . da-DA!)

"You're too much. I told you to stop hanging out there. Hookers do. Get smart, girl." Z adjusts the top of her bikini, trying to form cleavage with her double-A breasts. Futile. She's all nipples—like a Tom Wesselman nude. Z is constantly lifting weights. Futile. "You know," she says, "there's a rumor that Mick is replacing the director of the film you're up for, honey chile. So you better be good. How was he? A ten?"

"I don't remember."

"Sure. Later. I made it with Johnny Jordan in this room just last week." A sly smile crosses Z's full lips.

"How'd you manage that?" I ask. Eric is a maniac at jealousy.

"Eric was modeling at one of those Diedas conventions in Chicago. He was showing his beautiful feet in sneakers. I was showing our beautiful house to Johnny, and he looked the whole thing over with interest. Being in real estate does have its advantages."

"Did Johnny leave his boots on?"

"You gotta cough up Mick first, dearie."

"You know I always tell you everything."

"Ssh! I hear Eric's famous feet."

A bicep-bulging, grinning Eric Sargeant, wearing red socks and short white trunks with the Diedas label on a hip pocket, slowly walks toward me. His smooth, deeply tanned skin is covered with a greasy suntan oil, and so is his hair, now golden from the sun. His brown, blazing eyes study my body. His arms wrap around me as though he were going to undo the top of my bikini. I feel his warm chest press against mine. His lips move toward mine. I offer him my cheek. He pulls away.

"Well, if it isn't our favorite piece of pulchritude for the great big role in *The Starlet*. You are yawning early, Maya. Are you getting up or going down?"

"It's too early for repartee, Eric. I need sustenance."

"Come with me. My people by the pool will give you sustenance."

I shake my head. With a hangover and without a drink, the pool is not for me. It's too bright out there. I ask for the bar.

Z grabs my hand and leads me to the kitchen. There, an older woman in a black apron pours freshly blended margaritas. (She's shaky too. This morning, all the world's a hangover.)

On the way to the pool I whisper to Z, "Your maid's about to cry."

"That's my mother."

"What? Your mother's your maid?"

"Don't judge me, Maya. If your mother was a drug addict and tried to stab you when you were a kid, how would you feel? She's always threatening to kill herself." Z pulls a tiny pillbox out of the top of her bikini and pops a yellow capsule.

I swallow a quick swig of tequila and feel sorry for Z. Maybe she wants a cuddle just like me. I wonder how a Mormon can be a drug addict.

"Hey, Z, I'm sorry. Guess I didn't tell you everything about my mom either." I want to ask if her mother forced enemas on her. But the timing is bad, and I can't say that word, "enema."

Nervously, Z grabs my hand and leads me out to the dozen guests seated at several round white Abbey-Rents Formica tables topped by colorful umbrellas.

"Folks, this is Maya Endicott. Maya, meet Darian Nelson and Don Larski, Diane Carter and Joe Marino. He's Italy's number one male model." Z gets bored with this. "The rest of you," she announces, "are not important."

Laughter all around.

"FUCK YOU TOO, ZO-EEE," shouts a plump man in a three-piece seersucker suit.

"GO HAVE YOUR TEETH REWIRED, MARVIN," Z screams back.

I must still be full of stodgy old Philadelphia. They seem awfully crass. I need lessons. But I do my best to smile along with the rest. I am even thinking in doggerel. I take a few more quick sips of Mexico's finest.

Darian Nelson. Can my eyes be true? She is covered from her gorgeous blond head to her lovely toes in a white kaftan, with enormous shoulder pads. Why? It's a hot sunny day, and she has the very best body in the world. In fact, now that I notice, they all seem to be hiding their bodies from the sun. A glorious kidney-shaped swimming pool is within diving distance, and not one splasher in it.

I squeeze into a chair next to Eric. I feel safe with him. And I adore him when he makes fun of himself.

For a change, I try to listen. I hear gossip and more gossip. My sunglasses help me conduct a scar search. Rumor has it that Darian is all plastic. A few of her ribs, the secret story says, were removed to create her fabulous cleavage. Her over-forty chin is very tight. Everyone's chin is tight, except for Marvin's. Marvin is red-faced and shouting one-liners. "HEY, ZO-EEE, SO WHERE'S YOUR CLEAVAGE? THOUGHT YOU WERE LIFTING WEIGHTS?"

Boring. A quiet June Anthony appears to be listening intently to everyone's shriek and slop. Probably memorizing dialogue for her next potboiler. How can everyone be so accepting of her? Courageous June wrote a best-seller exposing Hollywood's back door, *The Hollywood Club*. Success, no matter how, no matter where, is what these people worship. God, I hope I get that part.

Joe Marino, not more than thirty, is all over Diane, who is nearly two decades older than he. He fondles her clasped hands, which are covered in rings of all sizes. Claws in diamonds. Dare

I say hello to Joe and recall that blind date we had in Rome six months ago? He was driving a battered Honda Civic and tried to force his way into my room at 4 A.M. Can't he say hello to me now? No, I rejected him.

I don't belong.

Darian has the spotlight. What confidence! That I envy. I remember when I first saw her—in a disco, the Voom Voom, in Cap d'Antibes. She was performing a solo go-go dance in a brief mini and tiny pasties. Her look was poor tack and her tanned olive skin gave her the appearance of a Puerto Rican or mulatto. She claims she is of American Indian descent. She laughs. Her teeth are perfect. Lip gloss gleams in the sun. Her Joy perfume is more powerful than the scent of honeysuckle. She waves lacquered fingers in the air. "Last night I went to a party at Harry Blydon's. What an evening! He ran those screen tests for *The Starlet*. Horrible. Harry offered me three mill to do that same piece of schlock—I just had to undress, he said. I turned him down. But leave it to Harry. He dug up six eager beavers. There they were, naked, spread-eagled, chained to a bed. Naughty camera. Harry's looking for a beaver queen!" Darian taps her fingers on her terrycloth-covered thigh.

Marvin howls. Diane and June smile. Everyone has a good laugh.

I get up from my chair and head for the kitchen and fix myself another margarita. Z's mother has disappeared. Eric joins me.

I wrap my arms around his lean suntanned body and bury my head in his hairless chest.

"Maya, you're going to have to learn to laugh at Hollywood, or it will destroy you. And that would be your fault, your choice." Eric holds my chin in his hand and looks into my eyes. "It's attitude. This is a funny town. Play it like you would a game." He wipes my tears with a paper towel.

Z enters. Her beautiful blue eyes bulge. She feigns a yawn. "Maya, if I thought you fancied Eric, I might be worried."

Turning to Eric she laughs. "She's a star-fucker, darlin'. That leaves you out."

Eric clears his throat. "Tact, my sweet, is not why I married you. It's those magnificent blow jobs."

"You don't know what magnificent is," Z says, rolling her eyes toward the ceiling.

"Thanks, Eric. I needed the pep talk. My hangover's getting to me, Z. I'm splitting."

"Don't let Darian get you down. She didn't know you were one of those girls. Honest."

"Sure."

"Look, no one at the luncheon knows you tested for *The Starlet*. You're being paranoid, as usual."

"Hollywood takes some adjusting."

"That's right. And it's worth it. Don't make waves with the women in this town, Maya. The women run the men—the wives run the industry. Be careful. Darian can help you more than any man, so don't start thinking she doesn't like you. She's been where you are and knows how to make it all work. But she never hung out at the Hollywood Hills Hotel pool."

"I'm a New Yorker, Z. I like it there. It reminds me of the South of France. I see all my friends from Manhattan."

"Bet you get a lot of business cards too. You know you'll get a bad reputation. Don't come crying to me when you lose a part because someone thinks you're a hooker in from the East. You're selling sex on the screen, not at the pool, fuck-face."

"You remind me of my mother."

"Sorry about that. Talk to you tomorrow. I must get back to the A group. And next luncheon leave your eye makeup home. Men don't like too much in the day. Oh, you need so many lessons, honey, but I love ya all the same. Your wonderful spirit. Even though you are a douche bag!"

"Yes, Mom." I head toward my Fiat and am home in one side of a cassette.

My cottage seems like a palace. I turn on my neon sculptures and my stereo. Tutu needs food. I'm grateful to have him even if he belonged to my former fiancé, the creep. The creep I love. Or thought I loved? Tutu is worth every bit of the six years I spent with his master.

I give Tutu some biscuits and pour myself a gin and tonic. I am sick. The film studio promised me that the screen tests would be locked in a vault. Instead they're being flashed around the Bel Air circuit. I am fodder for at-home porno flicks for the moguls and the stars. Seven years of acting lessons. Is this what my New York agent was trying to tell me? I hope this town isn't as grim as advertised. Darian Nelson and Diane Carter (they've been around the block!) must have dealt with this sort of male behavior. And they're smiling today.

I try to rally. I feel that tingling sensation. Buzzing. No. Not now. Not here. Not in Hollywood. I see the face of that cab driver, other faces.

A stronger drink. That will do it. I pour more gin. As I throw down my drink, I begin to feel better. Relaxed. What cab driver? I laugh.

I like Z. And Eric. I have a couple of friends. I am somewhat of a celebrity in my own right. After all, 1,500 girls were interviewed for this film. I am a finalist. What's wrong with nudity? When I modeled I was photographed in the nude for Toyota. When I studied figure drawing at the U. of P., I worked from a model who only wore a Tampax. When I tested for a major motion picture, I was filmed in the nude. And what of it? I am proud, I tell myself.

Well, Mother, again this is one of those things you don't have to know. A perfect body may be exposed. Yes, all of it. From A to P.

6

CASTING for *The Starlet* was delayed one month, bringing even more attention to the film. Acting classes, gym classes and men occupy my time. "There's a New Girl in Town" is a popular tune in the land of the rising star.

On Valentine's Day, Z invited me to a party welcoming an English producer, Alexander "Sacha" Shactel, to Hollywood. Eric was at a Diedas convention in Chicago working his feet off. Sacha had a reputation for discovering famous beauties and turning them into stars. His terms were steep. It was rumored that he was the king of kink, but what that meant few knew.

I grabbed my black Christian Dior that made my cleavage even more likely to become famous, pulled on black stockings with seams running up the sides, stepped into my black satin and rhinestone ankle straps, drenched myself in perfume and dried my hair in my convertible, top down of course. Z and I met at the Arco station on Sunset. I would follow her. I could never walk into a party alone.

I loved driving up Coldwater Canyon at night, passing the tall pine trees that stood proudly under the moonlight like dark green giants guarding the road. Four men with flashlights signaled for us to pull over. A red and white metal sign saying Valet Parking stood off to one side. We gave our cars to the attendants, moonlighting male models looking to be made into movie stars by someone whose car they parked. They were also taking notes with their ears to sell to gossip columnists in the A.M. When guests left a party, they had to wait outside with the valets for their cars to be delivered, and of course everyone—stars, agents, managers, directors—bragged at the mouth, dished, shot the shit, commented on what had happened at the party.

As Z and I walked up the flagstone path to the rambling estate of Jeffrey Dawson, manager of the stars, we smelled a strong repulsive odor.

"Ekk!" Z said, pulling up her long burgundy taffeta skirt to avoid a steady flow of water coming down the hill. "What's that?"

"Smells like the inside of an outhouse!" I said, knowing the stench well since my grandparents had had an outhouse on their farm in Pottstown, Pa.

A man behind us chuckled. "Guess Jeffrey's sewage backed up again."

"Jesus," Z said, frowning. "Why doesn't he call a plumber instead of giving a party?"

It felt as if we had trudged a mile from the Valet Parking, and through a sewer at that. Was this Hollywood's idea of glamour?

Jeffrey Dawson's stone mansion appeared to have a bedroom for each of his fifty invited guests. A friendly waiter holding a tray of glasses filled with red and white wine greeted us just inside the door.

The smoke-filled room was crowded with standing bodies more concerned with talking than with listening. I had trouble hearing Z. "Just push your way through the masses, m'selle. Use your elbows. It's called the Hollywood shuffle."

No one paid attention to me. Usually when I dressed in an outfit this revealing, I was noticed, at least by men. Though my name had gained notoriety because of the sensationalism of my screen test for *The Starlet*, the good folk of Hollywood did not know what Maya Endicott looked like in the flesh—hence I was ignored. I focused on Mr. Dawson's art collection: posters from movies and photos of movie stars. All his clients? Dark brown walls and dark hardwood floors gave a somber feeling to the living room. Over a fireplace filled with cardboard logs hung the massive head of a buck proudly flaunting his antlers to Hollywood. He seemed to smile at me. I returned the smile, the first of the night. I looked around the room at what the guests were wearing—some women in fancy dresses, others looking like they had come from the office, men in cords and jeans, lots of T-shirts.

Z had disappeared into the sea of elbows. I stared back at Mr. Buck with a twinge of envy, then took another glass of wine from a passing waiter.

Harry Blydon, the producer of *The Starlet*, was the only person to introduce himself. He knew too well what I looked like. Short, pudgy and with that mogul moustache and L.A. guess-what-I'm-hiding beard, he said in thick Brooklynese with a glint in his eyes, "Miss Endicott, I was on location when you were tested. But I wanna let you know—before you get your hopes up"—and his eyes shifted—"you won't be starring in *The Starlet*. Your tits, Ms. Gorgeous, are too small, and you are too classy. However, your test was the best. The finger-lickin' best."

I swallowed my tears along with my white wine, which would help me to smile. I wasn't going to give up. It was a long way to Philadelphia, but it looked pretty good right now. My voice was high and strained. "Well, Mr. Blydon, I'm sorry that I'm not right. But could I see the test? It means a lot to me. I could drop by your office."

He put his hand in his pants pocket. Change rattled. "I'd be delighted to show you yourself on film. How about tomorrow? End of the day? I'm busy earlier editing *The Texas Hand*."

"Oh, that's kind, Mr. Blydon."

"Harry. Call me Harry."

"Great, Harry," I said while adjusting my bodice. His eyes went right into the well of my cleavage.

He was going to be easy, I thought. Tits too small? We'll see.
They had been in high school. I wore a padded bra, two pairs of
bobby sox and drank heavy cream. My nickname was Toothpick! At college, away from Mom and disfigured Dad, I
sprouted tits! Plenty of them! Today my tits weren't too small
for any man.

"*A demain*, Har-ry," I said, and turned to get more wine.
Where was Z? I needed Z for a conference. She'd tell me how to
handle this creep.

The party was packed with agents, managers, and lesser
types with heads that could twist 360 degrees. No one lesser
wanted to miss anyone better; therefore everyone had to be
missing someone. My drink (my rod and my staff) comforted
me. Great, Harry.

Z was talking to Sacha Shactel. Wouldn't you know. The girl
didn't miss a trick. Sacha was short, fat, had bulging eyes and
was sixty-four! Alexander "Sacha" Shactel. A distant cousin to
Harry Blydon. I signaled Z to join me in my corner of the ornate den.

As Z pulled herself away, Sacha kept staring at me. People
milled around him, but he was concentrating his attentions my
way. Still, I needed Z. One producer at a time, I told myself.
Hurry up, Z!

"You dildo, why didn't you come over?" Z smiled. "Sacha
seems mad about you."

"Harry Blydon. He's going to show me my test tomorrow
night in his office."

"Don't worry about Blydon. Work on Sacha. He likes ladies
who dress up. Tomorrow hit Frederick's. Get the kinkiest underwear. Sacha won't be running around in your high heels like
Herr Blydon."

Before I could digest all this, Sacha Shactel was offering me a
Sherman. "Miss Endicott, I've heard great things about your
work. Call me at my office tomorrow. I'd like to discuss a
project with you."

There was actual kindness coming out of his Paul Newman–

blues. They stripped me of my defenses. I liked fat Sacha instantly. How nice. I also liked what he could do for me.

"Please call me Maya. I have an audition tomorrow. Could we make it the day after?"

"If you're free for lunch, we could meet at La Scala. One o'clock?"

"Terrific." Sacha released my hand. A pushy agent shoved his hand into Sacha's. Time to split.

Z kissed Sacha on his round cheek and whispered something in his ear. His eyes blazed.

I retreated to the bar. I needed liquid relaxation, and quick. It gave me the ability to appear glib when my insides were slum full of fear.

Noon. Next day. Z's bedroom. Mirrors covered three of the four walls as well as the ceiling. An Erté poster and photos of Z in various costumes, as well as naked, decorated the remaining wall. Thick black carpeting that didn't show dirt (so Z boasted while complaining about the lint) cushioned my bare feet. Strewn on the bed was a black silk comforter with an Oriental motif. Underneath, wrinkled black satin sheets. On the shelf behind the bed Z's sex equipment was neatly laid out: a variety of feathers, corsets, garter belts, fringe, G-strings, bras with cutouts, love potions, Vaseline, pearls, ben-wa balls, a vibrator, chains, wrist cuffs, cock rings, Blistex and rubber gloves.

Z lay on the bed in faded jeans and a denim workshirt. A thick green paste covered her face; her hair was in rollers. I sat beside her.

"All right, girlie, first get a large hand mirror. Pretend it's your target. Give the mirror a name. Let's call it 'Harry,' as in Blydon. Fix your lighting the way it would be. If you're into candles, light them. The fewer the better. Unless he's nearsighted. If you're fucking Mr. Magoo, you gotta give him a view."

"Z, you're nuts."

"Make sure you don't have cross lighting on your face. On your body, great! But on your face it's aging. In the mirror check out your makeup, hairstyle, facial expressions—in all positions—and make choices just like you're doing a scene. Pick a hairstyle that looks good in bed, and give him a good view of your mouth. The best position for fucking and looking good is with the woman on the bottom. Great for bone structure when you're looking up at him. All that over-eighteen facial fat falls to the side."

"But, Z, I like to be on top."

"Well, dearie, do what ya gotta do, but adjust the lighting. When you're on top, throw your head back. That keeps the extra flesh from falling forward."

"But I like eye contact."

"Then look him in the eyes, but keep your chin up. It's like film. Imagine a key light over your head. At all times!"

"Too much to think about. How do you manage to let go?"

"Listen, lily white, you fake that. Fucking in Hollywood is all about looking good. Don't try to have orgasms with any of these guys. Sex is business out here."

"What do I do when I need sex?"

"Go to the gym, asshole, or grab a gardener. But don't have sex with a producer, director, actor, agent, studio head, head honcho, or anyone in the industry and look at it as anything but an audition. The name of the game is Casting Couch!"

"God, Z, you're so crass!"

"Cutie pie, I'm honest. Industry sex is hipped on performance. You fool yourself if you think it's anything else. The guys in this town carry power in their crotch. You wanna be a star? Please the power. Get passed around. You will be whether you like it or not, so you might as well accept it and do what you gotta do. Which is fuck, honey chile. Fuck those idiots good."

"I'm gonna need my pills for this, Z."

"Why do you think they were invented, luvvy? You'll puke if

you aren't loaded. But take them in moderation. Don't lose control completely. Because then you become a pawn."

"Yes, boss!"

"Always have some love potion—emotion lotion is good—tucked under your pillow. Or wherever you usually have sex. Stash a couple bottles around your apartment near your favorite sex furniture. When you're on call, make sure you have a vial in your handbag. Think of yourself as a night nurse doing duty."

"Emotion lotion?"

Z reached behind her bed for a yellow-tinted plastic bottle and squeezed its contents onto the palm of her hand. "This is pear-flavored. No other lubricant needed. Its light color doesn't stain or leave traces. Rub this stuff wherever your target wants tongue, kiddo. This saves you from asking Mr. Mogul to wash. Telling a honcho he stinks doesn't go over big in Hollywood. And this way you'll never know how dirty he really is and therefore won't feel bad about yourself."

"Z, this is a turnoff."

"Baby cakes, these guys are into degrading women. Part of their humiliation toolkit is pretending they don't know how to use a washcloth, dig?"

"Ekk!"

"Oh, I forgot masks. Get some. You'll find some of these guys are afraid. Masks help them to relax."

"Sounds like geisha training."

"Now as far as what to say. Dirty talk, filthy language, turns men on. Read a little pure unadulterated smut before each date."

"This is work!"

"Do you think it's easy for a sex symbol to become a star? You are expected to know what you're doing, dollface. Now for the orgasm."

"I thought I wasn't supposed to have one."

"That's right. But you must learn how to simulate one. Go to the zoo. Listen to hyenas. Study animal sounds. If you're not into zoos, buy tapes. Think of yourself as a cat in heat. Wailing sounds are good. Sighing and moaning are standard. Be different. Howl. Scare him a little. He'll remember you. And like it afterward. Howl again to let him know you're coming. Once you're through with the whole thing, you can go home and eat a clove of garlic."

"I don't like garlic."

"Let me summarize. You'll be eaten up if you don't get a reputation as a good fuck. You want a director to want to take you on location."

"You've given me a headache."

"Enough lessons for one day. You have Harry Blydon tonight. Give it to him, kiddo. He doesn't love you, but I do."

I left Z's feeling sick. Who was the genius who said it is the truth that gives you nausea?

I still wanted to be a star.

'7

HARRY Blydon's executive suite on the first floor of the studio's administration building was the most prestigious spot on the lot. In fact, everything surrounding Harry was prestigious —even his trendy white *Chariots of Fire* cable-knit sweater. Harry's mother was a New York socialite, so Harry knew what went with what. Tortoiseshell glasses gave him a studious appearance.

"Want a hit?" he said, pointing a well-manicured finger to a line of cocaine on a mirrored tray.

"But of course." I inhaled these fine chemicals and fear took a walk.

Harry laid out more coke. "Help yourself. The supply's unlimited."

I dropped my cape over a mahogany chair. Bending over a mahogany desk, I inhaled again. And again. Harry seemed to be studying my lungs. For this audition I had decided to dress as though I were stepping out later in the evening (even though I wasn't). A black silk jersey that crossed over my breasts and tied at my hip with a sash. The skirt flared open when I crossed my knees. A working dress.

"Hot date?" Harry took a toot.

"A date."

"Well, Maya, you certainly have the equipment for the part. In these surroundings you look more perfect than ever."

I stared at a portrait of Irving Thalberg on the paneled wall. A green Tiffany lamp glowed.

"Maybe I could convince the studio that you aren't too classy for *The Starlet*. But first you'd have to convince me."

"But you said you want a more zoftig . . ."

"Opinions can be changed." I could feel Harry's breath on my lips. He removed his glasses. Gently he pulled at my sash. My dress fell open. There I was, naked with garter belt, stockings, high heels. No panties.

"Miss Endicott, the more I see of you the more you look like a heroine." Harry kissed my nipples, which hardened under his cocaine-coated tongue.

I was trying to think of what I liked about Harry. Difficult. I must concentrate. I had to be good! Z had warned me.

I liked his soft voice. It hummed. He had been an actor (once a starlet just like me).

"Now you're acting less like a producer, Mr. Blydon. Please don't stop."

Thin pasty lips pressed on mine. He yanked off his sweater, unbuttoned his oxford shirt (a freckled chest). Accidentally, his cocaine vial fell onto the Oriental carpet.

"My, I'm uncoordinated today," he said, slipping my dress off my shoulders. It fell to the floor. I turned around and bent over, straight-legged, to rescue the vial. Time passed. He had me posing. "Yes, Miss Endicott, you have what it takes. Don't move." I had no intention. I did have a passing thought—I wished I'd worn black lace gloves. Then a hand came between my cheeks. Dry fingers covered in white powder.

"Oh, Harry. What hands you have."

"Don't move, Miss Endicott. Coke does wonders everywhere."

Still bending spread-legged, I stared at the carpet. I was able to look between my legs at Harry. He was dropping his jeans. His boxer shorts. I was looking at naked Harry—without an erection. Undoubtedly he was a head man. Like most of Hollywood.

But now I was ready. Coke turned me on. I never cared who I was with. On coke, I could have sex with a Saint Bernard. Harry was the dog of my choice right now. I wanted to feel him inside me. Any man's hard-on. I loved to move men around in bed. Get them to do for me. Make them work for me. One lover called me the General. On coke, I could go for hours. I loved to exploit men, and I was in the right place. Hollywood.

Come on, Harry! Get it up for your country! Produce me, Harry! What good is a producer without a hard-on?

Harry embraced me. That is, he pulled me onto the rug. I grabbed him by his scrotum. It seemed the best choice since he still had no erection. He shoved my head into position. I did him. Circling. Stroking. Sucking. Licking. Thinking about instructions in various sex manuals I had read.

He moaned. "Oh, you're the best, baby." I hated to be called baby. He'd probably forgotten my name. Come on, Harry! I inserted a finger. Z had told me to keep my middle fingernail short at all times. Be prepared!

"Oh, God, up—oooh. Where did you learn to do that? Higher! Yes, that's beautiful, baby."

Still no erection. I pressed my middle finger upward inside Harry. "Oh, oh . . . OH!"

Suddenly he seized me. Mounted me. Rubbed my erection with his lack of one. Up and down. More moaning. Sighing. Acting as if he were about to come . . . having a great time. (Sure, Harry.)

He turned me over. Pressed my shoulders, pubic bone and face into the Oriental carpet. Again he mounted me, rubbing his dangling appendage up and down between my buttocks. "God, baby, you're something else. What an ass . . . oh, what you do to me."

Then I realized . . . why, Harry was auditioning for me!

A garbled cry. And from a limp Harry wetness shot onto my flesh and trickled down my backside. I glared at the portrait of Irving Thalberg. A premature ejaculator. Another Hollywood secret. The trouble with Harry.

His Limpness fell to the floor. I began to roll over when he shouted, "DON'T! YOU'LL STAIN THE CARPET!"

The following day I was cast to star in *The Starlet*.

On to lunch with Alexander "Sacha" Shactel.

AFTER Harry Blydon my cunt was beginning to feel like a hotel. With Sacha, I would be changing the sheets.

At least, I told myself, each big and limp little penis would be helping me to forget Jean-Paul.

I was fifteen minutes late for lunch, as usual. Always keep the power waiting—my motto. In Hollywood—so Z told me—everyone was so busy ass-licking, both figuratively and literally, that when producers, directors, mini and maxi moguls or honchos were insulted, they found it refreshing. And you gained a tinge of respect.

La Scala was, of course, crowded. The queue extended from the cashier out to the street. Sacha Shactel was sitting in the corner booth, the best in the place. He was on the phone, naturally. Every booth had a phone. Lunch was eaten with the fork in one hand and the phone in the other.

Sacha was wearing a three-piece navy blue pinstriped suit. I was wearing a burgundy silk shirtdress, trying to look like a lady. He stood and extended his hand.

"Oh, Sacha, please forgive me. Traffic is impossible."

A short, fat Sacha remained standing until I sat on the shiny red vinyl.

"You look like an Italian countess today, my dear. I love to see your forehead." (I usually wore my hair in bangs that looked like they had been caught in a blender.)

"I can't stand it this way. But my agent insists that I show my face."

"He's right. And you are wrong. This look is elegant. Elegance and sex are a rare combination. You should take advantage of your best feature." Sacha clasped his pudgy hands. A diamond ring adorned his pinky. Despite his reputation as a dirty old producer, there was an innocence and sweetness shining from his clear, light blue eyes. Again, all of a sudden, I liked him. I realized that, plump or not, he was actually handsome— even at sixty-four. After five minutes of listening to him, I forgot his age. I was beginning to feel safe with Daddy Sacha. All men wanted to fuck me, but not all men were nice to me. Sacha listened when I spoke.

"Miss Endicott, I would like to audition you for my film. But I must make the decision by tomorrow—financing, you see. Could you find time to read this afternoon, and audition for me later today?" Sacha held up a thick script.

"I was going to celebrate with my agent, Michael Stone. He didn't really get me this film, but he's going to handle my career from now on."

"Celebrate?"

"I was just cast as the lead in *The Starlet*."

"That's wonderful. Who's directing?"

"Jack René was replaced by Mick Hodges." (God, I was supposed to see him tonight—to thank him.)

"Ah, good . . . very good. You will be more desirable to my financiers. But first I must hear you read."

"My place or yours?"

"Wherever you feel comfortable. The lead wears a black corset most of the time. Louis Feraux will be doing the costumes. Remember Stanislavsky. Clothing first. Work on your characters from the outside in. This will help you get into the part." (I'd heard this speech somewhere before. I wondered if Sacha had seen my test for *The Starlet*.)

We made a date for nine at my place.

As we walked out of the restaurant, we passed Darian Nelson lunching with Zoe Sargeant. Z stopped everything to whisper in Sacha's ear.

He chuckled. "I like that."

God, she's rude, I thought. Not even a smile for me.

Fifteen minutes later, I was standing at a pay phone.

"Z, this is Maya."

"Hello, luvvy, some hot lunch. You make a real cute couple."

"What were you saying to Sacha about me?"

"Just turning Sacha on to you more. Don't get defensive, numb nuts. I put you two together."

"What did you say, Zoe?"

"Angel cakes, I won't be cross-examined."

"I won't have my sex life reamed around Hollywood."

"Look, don't bug me. Sacha does whatever I want him to. So fuck Sacha good. That's what I told him, kiddo, if you must know. That you were great in bed. But don't forget—work on your Kagel muscles."

"What?"

"Where have you been this semester? Vaginal muscles! Didn't I teach you this? Squeeze fifty times before each respectable fuck. Sacha's a pro. You don't want him slippin' and slidin'. You ain't exactly eighteen!"

"A fat sixty-four-year-old a good lover? Please!"

"My best sex ever was a week I had with a fat old man, my dear. You've turned on the big prize, but you're too small-minded to realize it."

"What fat old man, Z?" (Was it Sacha, I wondered.)

"That, whack job, is none of your business."

"But I tell you everything!"

"Your problem, big mouth. Learn discretion! Get out of the minor leagues. Gotta go, kiddo."

Click!

I didn't like the conversation.

Had Z told Sacha about that cab driver?

8 P.M., and the drums were beating for the gods of war. I put on my black lace corselette and black net stockings. I curled my hair, combed it with my fingers, grabbed a silver necklace and black lace gloves without fingers. Nails, Chinese red. And my black satin heels with rhinestone ankle straps. In the corset my waist measured eighteen inches and my thirty-seven-inch breasts popped over the stays like ammunition. (No G-string tonight!)

I was going to take advantage of my cottage's charm. When Sacha arrived, I would greet him in this outfit, show him my living room and climb ME FIRST to my tiny bedroom overlooking Laurel Canyon. A room with a view.

Tutu barked.

A knock at the door. I inhaled, squeezed my Kagel muscles, sprayed on more perfume. Damn! Z's phone conversation had thrown me. I'd forgotten to order pills from my dealer. No Ecstasy to pop tonight. No Quaaludes. No Purple Passion to turn me on. I was great on those pills. Scotch would have to do for a while. I opened the door. Tutu ran out to welcome Sacha.

He had changed into a black three-piece pinstriped suit. "My, my, who have we here?" he said as he petted Tutu.

"That's Monsieur Tutu. *Il est né à Neuilly.* He speaks French."

"Ah, *bon. Bonsoir,* Monsieur Tutu Endicott. How ravishing you look tonight, Maya."

"I decided to hide my forehead."

Instead of shaking my hand elegantly as he had at lunch today, he cupped his palms under each breast and kissed each nipple. He was undaunted. Tutu, as naked as his mistress, circled our feet. I felt flustered. I had thought I would intimidate Sacha.

Like a gentleman he now asked, "May I come in?" My body had been frozen in the doorway. His lips and tongue had felt good. General Endicott needed a drink.

"What would you like, Sacha?"

"I don't drink. Anything nonalcoholic."

What the fuck? Sacha didn't drink? Not possible. He was so chic. I poured myself a double scotch.

"Perrier?"

"Thank you. What a perfect body, Miss Endicott."

"So my mother's obstetrician said."

"I do wish we could have our lead wear that very outfit, but visible pubic hair would probably give us an X rating. All the same, you are a very lovely and abundant brunette." Sacha ran his hand between my legs and passed his fingers under his nose.

Tutu barked.

"*Il est jaloux*," said Sacha.

"*Mais oui.*"

"*N'y a pas de raison.*"

He was winning (hands down). I handed him his Perrier and poured another double scotch for the road to my bedroom. Warmth filled my body. I no longer felt uptight.

"Miss Endicott, do you like to ride?"

"Ride? *Mais oui.*"

He cleared his throat. "Horses."

"Oh, yes. I adore riding." (I'd ridden once.)

"*Bien*, the lead must be able to ride—topless—in one scene. There is a Lady Godiva chase."

"I haven't ridden for some time. I would need to work on my thighs."

"Perhaps you will come to my ranch in Santa Barbara next weekend? You could practice there."

"Why, I'd love to."

"Zoe and Darian have been. Many times. In fact they each have their own horse. Perhaps they would join us."

What? Zoe and Darian had their own horses? Had they both had affairs with Sacha? Were they still having affairs with Sacha? Z had better be telling me the truth.

We were still standing. I finished my drink and poured another. "Would you like to see the rest of my home?"

"Please." He gestured for me to lead. He knew what I had planned. I felt silly.

I held on to the railing and mounted the spiral stairs. Tutu followed.

"Are you coming, Sacha?" I said. I turned to see his expression. Sacha was staring at my buttocks.

"I'm following."

After a few more steps I finished my drink and looked back again. "*Qu'est-ce que c'est que ça, Monsieur Shactel?*"

"I am about to show you, *ma petite.*" Sacha's voice was low and determined, gravelly.

We reached the tiny treehouse-like bedroom with its mirrored wall behind a four-poster bed. Tutu jumped onto the rose satin sheets barking.

"Time for him to take a powder," I said, as I locked Monsieur Supertoots in the *salle de bain.*

"Must you?" Sacha asked.

"He'll eat your shoes. He's a fetishist. It runs in the family."

"What a perverse family you have. My family is much the same. But not for shoes."

I returned to the bedroom and sat on the edge of the bed. Legs spread, I lit a scented candle and switched off the lamp, longing for more scotch.

Sacha took off his jacket, undid his cufflinks and carefully placed them on the nightstand. He rolled up his sleeves, undid his tie, hung it on a bedpost, loosened his collar. "Now, precious. Let us hope I can show you what we've both been missing."

I lay back on the bed and dangled my feet over the edge like a high school nymphet waiting for that sweet boy who would first give her head. But this was a sixty-four-year-old kink king. We'll see, I thought. He better be good. To my horror I almost yawned.

"Perhaps you have some silk scarves?" Sacha asked.

"Silk scarves?"

"Yes."

"You'll find them in the top drawer."

"Lie with your pelvis on the edge of my bed, my beauty. That's right. Spread your legs as wide as you can. Good girl." He smiled. Sacha proceeded to tie one ankle to a bedpost, then the other.

Oh, my poor silk scarves. Now I was convinced he'd seen *The Starlet* test. He placed a pillow under my head. "This will afford you a better view." Like an expert gynecologist he knelt by the bed and began his examination.

He took his time. "What beautiful lips you have, Miss Endicott. You are so much like a very lovely flower—all purple and pink and . . . yes, dew." Sacha began massaging my thighs. He stopped short. Blew hot air over me. Saliva. He inserted the middle finger of his left hand into his mouth, then into me. He stared into my eyes, withdrew his finger and slid it back onto his tongue. He didn't blink. Didn't change his gaze. I watched. Waited. With the index finger of his right hand he began to rub my hood. Soon he replaced his finger with his mouth and tongue and teeth. Still gazing at me. I waited. I saw my hips begin to move upward against his tongue. Circling his face. He was concentrating, had closed his eyes. When I thrust my hips upward, he stared at me. I felt chained to his eyes. Time passed. Major surgery. I was letting go. I heard cries. Muffled cries. Heavy breathing. Garbled sounds. Like the ones Z had taught me to fake. I was breathing heavily. My muscles were volunteering all sorts of surprises. I felt suspended. Like foam. Confused. Who was this man? What was going on? What film was he making? I'd forgotten his name. More strange sounds. I was floating above. I felt good. Content. Like a star. More cries. Screams. Kicks.

"Shut up!" Sacha ordered in a low, raspy voice. I liked his voice. Loved it! It went right to my soul. It spoke the truth when he lied. It was that kind of voice.

I no longer cared who he was. What he said. What he could do for me. Where I was. I was covered in perspiration. Stomach muscles exhausted. I felt like a fountain.

When Sacha had finished penetrating every possibility of this position, he untied my legs, took off his vest, shirt, pants, socks, shoes, and now what appeared to be a very muscular and meaty, fair-haired thirty-nine-year-old placed his lips on mine. His face was wet, covered in my juice. His lips felt like magic. Soft, wise, sensitive, in control and full of surprises. I had never felt lips like Sacha Shactel's.

All the while he talked to me. Told me I'd make a great pornie star . . . if I wanted that. He would produce me. Take care of me. He stood next to the bed, spread my legs on either side of his head and gently moved in and out. In and out. Roughly in and out. Gently. Roughly. All the while staring into my eyes. Tears fell onto the sheets (mine).

More screaming.

"Shut up, I said."

More screaming.

"Shut up or I'll clip you."

More screaming.

Sacha shoved his fist into my stomach.

I liked it. My mother hit my father when she caught him reading dirty books. Dirty books were bad. I was bad. I liked to be hit. Sacha knew it.

"Stop moving. Stop! Or I'll come," he cried.

I obeyed. Awaiting direction. He was leading. I wanted him to. He made funny faces.

"Oh . . . I'm so hot. Wait!"

Breathing heavily, he joined me on the bed. "And now, my dear, it is your turn."

I began to mount him.

"No...NO!"

"What?"

"Suck me!"

"But I like to be on top." Then I could make men come and get it over with. I didn't want to fall in love. I didn't want Sacha to have any more of me. He had too much of me already. I wanted it to end. I pushed myself back on top of him and threw my breasts into his face.

"You heard me!" he shouted. I couldn't manipulate him. He was on to my game. Damn!

He shoved my head onto his cock. It was crimson. And so thick. Like a weapon. I hated to give head. I always felt so inferior. A failure. My first boyfriend told me I was useless at it. I was nineteen. He'd been seeing a hooker. "She was terrific," he'd tell me, and repeat how pathetic I was. But I kept trying. I had to learn. It was part of a girl's repertoire. I was all right when I didn't care about the man. But when I did, panic! I wanted an expert's certificate: "You are a worthy cocksucker, Ms. Endicott." But I never knew if the men were pretending to enjoy it. Like I usually was. With Sacha I wasn't pretending. No need.

I copied what I had just learned from him. Screw the fucking manuals! Sacha looked down at me. I looked into his eyes. I felt embarrassed. Did he know? I felt ashamed. God, if he knew what a truly un-tough act I was. Corset and black gloves, but for the payoff, no one home. My father would understand.

He began to moan. I didn't believe him. He sounded good anyway. His head was back on the pillow. That was a relief. I hated eye contact at this moment. I moved my head faster and faster. I remembered to grab his balls...gently at first...I think that's what men like. Or did Z say rough? Better be gentle and not make a mistake. I kept my finger deep inside him. This I knew how to do. It seemed easy next to the rest of the complexities of oral sex. He groaned.

Then he pulled my head off his cock. "Stop, I'm about to come. Wait!"

"Don't you want to come?" I asked, confused. Most men wanted to come in my mouth.

"Not yet." We'd been making love over an hour.

"Let's do some sixty-nine. Now you can audition." He grinned.

I didn't.

Sacha was exhausting me. But we did some sixty-nine. He shoved himself into my mouth. Silence. More pleasure. I couldn't take it. The more I gave up, the more I came. I felt like a hydrant.

He mounted me again. Out for blood. Mine. Z was right. She was always right. Had she fucked him? My mind shouted, Shut up! Enjoy this! It was always my goddamn mind that kept me from orgasms. Thinking. Thinking. Thinking.

Didn't he know I was old? Thirty-three is old to be an aspiring sex symbol in Hollywood. Who was I kidding? Is this what Z had whispered to him?

Sacha began moving inside me. Slowly, then deep, hard thrusts . . . then slow . . . then hard . . . whatever I least expected. Always looking into my eyes. Never blinking. Never glancing away. No longer talking. A magnet seemed to pull on my womb. As his penis developed a mind and rhythm of its own, his fingers massaged us both. I couldn't hold back. "I love you, Sacha," I heard myself say.

"You don't know me."

"Yes, I do."

"You don't."

"Know what?"

"You don't know what love is."

"Oh . . . Sacha. Don't." I closed my eyes and screamed. Someone was being murdered. Some part of me. I felt a knife shoot through me. My cunt. A wet knife. A liquid knife. A white-hot knife. I wanted that knife. I sucked. Squeezed. Grabbed Sacha under his balls. Slapped his ass with a cupped hand. Harder. Harder. He moaned. He shouted. His eyes lost focus. It felt like we rolled up to the ceiling.

Over.

9

I was in love with Sacha Shactel. It didn't make sense. But men never made sense.

Now what? When he left he said, "I'll call you." How long would he keep me waiting? Like a slave.

He was worth it. No one had ever made love to me like that. No one had ever made love to me. For one and a half hours Sacha had given me head. One and a half hours! With the men I'd been having sex with I was lucky to get ten minutes. And eight minutes of those ten were usually spent giving them head! Or trying to.

Why couldn't I tell these men how I felt? What I wanted?

I just couldn't. That's why.

That's why I drank and took pills. This combination did the talking for me.

But with Sacha I hadn't taken a pill and I'd had the best sex ever. He wouldn't let me control him. He controlled me and turned me on as powerfully as my flashing turned on men. But did he remain detached like I did with my victims?

I would have to keep busy. More than ever I was happy to be doing the lead in *The Starlet*.

The next day Sacha sent a dozen roses. A note asked if I was free for dinner that Sunday, Chasen's night.

When we entered the restaurant, he was given the best booth. I did not feel flippant or self-assured. No longer in control. I needed a nice strong mai-tai. Confidence on the rocks. Sex to the side, now I would have to talk and listen. Be intelligent, be a lady.

I felt as inferior in this role as in cocksucking. Oh, I had tried to learn to be funny. But court jesters weren't ladies. I never learned the fifty-seven cooler varieties of feminine grace.

After a mai-tai or two, I felt graceful, however, and very much a lady. And beautiful in my low-cut black cocktail dress.

"Perhaps you would like to go to the ballet one evening?" Sacha asked. His hair shone silver in the candlelight.

"That would be lovely."

"Do you like ballet?"

"Yes." (I didn't know a thing about it. In fact I found it boring.)

"Which is your favorite?"

"I don't have one. My mother took me to see *The Red Shoes*. After that I always wanted to jump in front of subways or be a ballerina—except in second grade I came down with rheumatic fever and wasn't allowed to dance."

"So you never went to the ballet again?" Sacha asked.

"Something like that." Stupid. Not only was I unable to talk about ballet, I felt unable to talk at all.

I ordered another mai-tai.

Sacha didn't seem to mind the silence. "When you come to Santa Barbara, bring along a good book. I enjoy reading in bed. Do you?"

"Yes." I never read in bed. I never read. I watched TV, listened to rock 'n' roll, talked on the telephone. Read? Who could concentrate?

Sacha held my hand under the table. "Have you ever read Proust?"

"Some Proust," I lied.

"My dear."

I downed my mai-tai.

"Darling." Now Sacha kissed me on the cheek. "Don't pretend with me. I like you as you are." Did he mean what he said? I wanted him to love me. Not like me, love me.

"I feel like an intellectual klutz with you, Sacha." Should I have been so revealing, I wondered.

"My dear, sometimes you are so silly." He squeezed my hand and now held it on top of the table. "My father was a gambler. He would walk into a room in his spats and charm the jewels off the wealthiest woman. Eventually he'd strip her of her riches."

"Was this before your mother?"

"Before, during and after." Sacha wiped his top lip with his napkin, then neatly folded it on his lap. "My father was irresistible. The most elegant con man. My mother paid for his dishonesty." Sacha's smile disappeared. "So please don't ever lie to me."

"Why didn't your mother leave him?"

"She threatened to once. Every time he lost at gambling or the mob tried to collect, there would be a terrible altercation. The next day there was always some big change. Not for the better. One day my mother said she was leaving. Of course taking me with her." Sacha finished his Perrier. "But I asked her to stay and she did."

Poor Sacha, I thought. "How old were you then?"

"Twelve. After the gambling stopped, my father began drinking. There were always women. My mother tolerated the situation as best she could."

Now I only loved Sacha more. Maybe I could make him feel better. I would have to accept his womanizing. Difficult. "Is that why you don't drink?"

"Partly. I did drink. I had a severe problem with alcohol, but I beat it."

"How?"

"I just stopped one day. Willpower."

I thought my mother would like Sacha, if she could get

beyond his age. Willpower. That's something I'd always been missing.

That night we made love again. Again it was good. Can I use "very"? I was drunk, and I should have been out of it, but it was very good. What I remembered, anyway.

The next morning I had a wardrobe fitting at the studio. Hung over, I was glad I wasn't filming. Tutu's walk was a detour—to his favorite tree and back. This A.M. he was not smiling as usual. By ten o'clock I had arrived at the office of Sam Matthews, head of wardrobe for Zercon Films deep in the heart of Burbank. I liked to drive onto the studio lot, past the different sets: ghost towns, country villages, old New York, stagecoach settings, the backdrop of a sky half a mile wide and fifty feet high, the famous actors walking about in wardrobe drinking sodas, the tour buses driving around, the passengers pointing at the famous actors in wardrobe drinking sodas. I liked to hear the sounds of honking, bells ringing, to see the flashing red lights signaling all quiet on a soundstage. Zercon Films had thirty-five stages; it was the biggest of all the studios in Hollywood.

Sam Matthews's office was a two-story white frame cottage on the back lot. A gray-haired man who could have been Sacha's bearded double sat in a rocking chair smoking a pipe. I loved that smell of chicory.

"So you're Maya Endicott." Sam stood and shook my hand, holding it a bit longer than necessary. He then took my measurements, holding the tape over my breasts a bit longer than necessary. "Would you try these few things, Maya? I want to get an idea of how you look in this neckline."

"Of course," I said, smiling. Sam's face was flushed. He returned to his desk and continued with his paperwork.

I looked around for a fitting room. "Where should I change?"

"Right there is as good a place as any. No point in being modest, Maya. We have to work together . . . what? eight weeks?

And you're naked in half the film."

He did have a point. Nevertheless, I felt this was unpro-
fessional. I walked behind a rack of clothes and whistled,
looking around the room as I slipped off my baggy sweater
and jeans. There were rows of period costumes, ball gowns,
outfits from different countries. One section had a row for
each of the last twenty years, with a hundred costumes per
row. I realized the cottage was the façade of an enormous
warehouse which stocked all the studio's wardrobe. Another
Hollywood façade.

As I changed, I peered over the rack at Sam, who was sneak-
ing peeks at me. The dress was low and tight. When I stepped
out from my shelter, Sam looked up. "I see you will need the
next size," he said, pulling up his trousers. "You can take it off
now." Sam returned to his paperwork red-faced. Slight beads of
perspiration covered his temples. He had three moles on his face
and long white hairs protruding from his nose. Sacha didn't
have these. If he did, he tweezed them. And Sam had a peculiar
body odor, like dirty feet. Sacha smelled like a wheat field after
the rain.

Well, that was painless, similar to the fittings I'd had when I
modeled. So often the client was a horny voyeur. Sam would be
easy to handle.

The next afternoon I met with my agent. The Michael Stone
Agency was on La Cienega Boulevard by the Santa Rosa car
wash, the car wash of the stars. Its four high-tech offices, con-
taining two sub-agents and a secretary, were on the second floor
of an old high-rise. Michael had invited Supertoots as well. Living in California was casual, relaxed. Anyone in a hurry was
ostracized. Laid-back was the behavior; soft-spoken, the voice;
streaked blond, the hair.

"Yes, put some streaks in your hair, Maya," a suntanned Michael said. "In low light, brown hair photographs like a hat.
Streaks make up for lousy lighting. Good lighting takes time,
and time is money."

"But when I modeled, I was told never to put anything on my hair. Processing ruins it."

"You're not a dim-witted model anymore, Maya. You're a movie star," Michael said, smiling.

Tutu didn't like Michael's attitude and lifted his leg on the saucer of a rubber plant behind him.

I gave Tutu a dirty look. He gave me one back. Michael, now sniffing the air, sat at a Formica desk with photos of his clients —mostly men—behind him. My photo was that glossy eight-by-ten in the string bikini that Jacques René had liked. "Have David Mann do some head shots. Look at this résumé to see if it's correct. The few lies are standard for a new actress," Michael said, smiling.

Why should I lie? Michael was so nice, he believed in me, so I didn't argue.

Tutu began sniffing Michael's corduroy-covered leg.

"Does your little darling have to do that?" Michael said, smiling.

"*Viens ici*, Tutu," I said, and he jumped in my lap.

"Oh, he speaks French. *Vous êtes mignon*, Monsieur Tutu."

Tutu growled.

"*Tais-toi*," I said. What was wrong with him?

With his crew cut, sandy hair, amber eyes and denim button-down shirt, Michael looked like he had just graduated from Princeton, but he told me he had never gone to college. "Waste of time. Don't tell clients, though. Maya, join a comedy workshop. Funny is money! Learn to do characters improvisationally, on your feet. Somebody who looks like you and can be funny is worth a million bucks."

Tutu started panting.

"Join a gym. The Sports Connection. Casting directors go there. And in your social life, be discreet. Most actresses who make it—you *do* want to make it, Maya?—avoid parties. Stay away from men. Play with your dog at night," Michael said, smiling.

Tutu snapped at Michael's hand.

"Ornery little cuss. He's just being French," Michael said, smiling, looking for tooth marks.

"Now that's about it. Oh, could you have dinner *chez moi* tomorrow night? Nathan Travis, the chairman of the board of Zercon Films, is coming as well. You might like him."

Tutu and I left Michael feeling a bit confused. We took a walk up La Cienega. I needed one. If my agent wanted me to stay away from the men in the industry, why did he want me to come to dinner with the chairman of the board of Zercon Films?

The following morning Michael called to cancel my invitation to dinner. Nathan Travis couldn't make it.

The week before *The Starlet* began filming I couldn't sleep. Typical. Before any big modeling assignment I'd always had to have eight hours' rest to look good.

Starring in a movie and having to be up at five A.M. for eight weeks made my fear of sleep humongous. Furthermore, when Jacques René was sacked and Oscar-winning director Mick Hodges was hired, Zercon Films tripled the budget, which now tumbled in at $25 million. Harry Blydon had been fired and replaced by Cloris Rudman, who was known for her interest in women's rights. Jane Webb, a Pulitzer Prize winner, had replaced the former screenwriter, who had been delivering drafts late because of his severe drinking problem. Now with a woman producer and a woman screenwriter the film's focus had changed from one of sexploitation to one of a sex symbol finding her identity through her struggle to survive in a male-dominated environment—the bedroom.

Why hadn't I been fired? I didn't know a thing about women's rights, nor did I really care. Well, I cared about my rights, but I wasn't too concerned about anybody else's.

The Starlet had the possibility of becoming a class project—but the nudity remained. This film would get a lot of attention. Zercon Films was trying to bust Hollywood's double standard about sex and create a big-budget film with a European flavor.

Even the men were going to be naked—totally, from all angles. Equal frontal exposure. No jockstraps. No black gaffer's tape stuck on men's genitals to photograph as shadow. (I fantasized about being in on that casting session.)

Did Zercon Films really know who they hired when they cast me? Surely sleeping with Mick Hodges wasn't the reason I was cast. Or was it? I'd never make it through the eight weeks looking gorgeous and fresh each morning, remembering my lines, not picking a fight with someone, feeling alert at five A.M.

Only five days before the shooting was to begin, one of the four male leads, who was playing the role of a truck driver, quit. He would not do the required nudity. (It was rumored that he felt he had too small a penis.)

A casting session was called, and I was to read along with the men; my fantasy had come true.

The story of *The Starlet*, rather than its actors, was to be the focus of the movie, so the search was on for an unknown male talent. Because unknowns rarely had film to show of themselves and because shooting was to begin in days, the men would be asked to strip and do the scene in the nude as they would in the film.

Cloris Rudman, wearing her gold-wire glasses and a navy linen suit, sat beside Jane Webb, in jeans and a T-shirt, on the brown leather sofa of a small windowless office on the eleventh floor of Zercon Films' executive tower. Mick Hodges, also in T-shirt and jeans, was to supervise the auditions.

"Let's remember, ladies—and Mick—how we hate being abused in a situation like this," producer Rudman said, inhaling deeply. "Let's treat these men the way we expect to be treated—with respect."

Mick Hodges coughed. Jane Webb giggled. I thought, This is going to be fun. Why hadn't Cloris been the producer when I tested?

"Maya," Cloris said, "I think you'll feel less awkward in your bikini once we begin."

"No problem," I said, grateful I didn't have to be naked as well.

Mario Mendoza, tall, green-eyed, black-haired and built like he had stepped out of a cave a millennium ago, was the first actor.

"I've been at the Neighborhood Playhouse for three years," he said in a deep voice that emerged from thick, perfectly formed lips. "Before that I waited tables. That's it."

For me, that was enough. His tight dark skin looked like a Polynesian appetizer.

"Your agent, I believe, told you how this scene was to be read," Mick Hodges said, "so if you'll take . . ." As Mick spoke Mario was stripping and staring at Cloris, who fumbled with her notes. Mario unzipped his fly, stepped out of his jeans and then studied Jane Webb, who was having an attack of hay fever.

Seated behind him, I couldn't help noticing his high, firm buttocks. My face reddened.

Mario didn't flinch. Cloris and Jane were now both coughing into Kleenex as Mario stood with his legs spread and his wrists clasped behind his back.

Mick cleared his throat and said, "That's fine, Mario. Now turn around, please." A completely naked Mario turned my way with a hint of an erection. His tan skin had white marks where his jockstrap-like swimsuit had been. From this whiteness masses of black pubic hair hung like Spanish moss. "Fine, Mario," Mick said without emotion. "Now I want to introduce to you our star, Maya Endicott."

Mario stood in front of me and extended his arm. I looked into his green eyes and reached out, terrified I'd grab something I shouldn't. His hand was just in front of his award-winning semi-erect self. He smiled, white teeth glistening, dimples creasing.

"Now, Mario, sit," Mick said as though he were directing Lassie. "Please begin with the scene where you rape Maya."

Seconds after he left, Mario was cast. Jane Webb sighed, looking as though she had been gang-banged, while Cloris Rudman loosened the first two buttons of her blouse and said, "I don't have the stamina to go through another casting session. How do men do it?" Mick Hodges laughed, and I looked forward to developing a good working relationship with Mario.

Cameras began to roll on *The Starlet* the middle of March. My five-minute crush on Mario ended when I realized Mario was in love with Mario. So was another male lead. The other two had cases on themselves as well. Four naked men and me—and no thrills, not even cheap ones.

During filming I saw Sacha once a week. We never got to Santa Barbara. I filmed in the day, and at night, with the help of a bottle of wine, worked on my lines. Mick Hodges kept calling. I put him off. I had the part, but didn't regret our brief sexual encounter. I felt safe with his direction, and didn't feel he was trying to get me into bed, because he already had. Some days he was getting a performance out of me. No sexual experience was entirely in vain.

The first six weeks seemed to go smoothly. Then the movie became work, and Sacha became the obsession.

I began having trouble memorizing the script. Every day it was up at 5:00. Wash hair. Walk Tutu. 5:45 pick-up. 6:00 arrive on set. Makeup. Study dialogue. Hair set. Electric rollers burn scalp. Study dialogue. Facial exercises. Mouth the

words. To the mirror. To myself. Make choices. Back to
makeup. Finishing touches. Fight about eyeliner. Study dialogue. To wardrobe. Sexpot's outfit. Stuffed Barbie doll.
Mouth that dialogue. Pushed onto set in Carmen curlers. Tits
half exposed.

Twelve noon. Lunch! Thank God for the thermos of Bloody
Marys which I brought to the set during the final weeks of filming. Vodka was tolerance. Occasionally I would overindulge and
feel like a voodoo doll—stuck with a million pins. On those
days making a movie was like volunteering for internment camp.
By the time I finished my thermos I felt like everyone's victim.
The director, the cameramen, the lighting crew, the scriptwriter
("Don't change my lines"), the hairdresser, the makeup artist,
the wardrobe mistress.

One night, alone, after work, I decided to call Z. Since our
last conversation, I'd been avoiding her like herpes.

"Hi, sweetpea. How's Sacha Shactel's sex kitten doing in the
litter box?"

"Z, I had no idea acting was so tedious."

"Fifteen hundred women auditioned and you're bitchin'."

"Give me the dish on Sacha."

"Falling for the stud?"

"Something like that."

"You're not gonna like it."

"Please tell me, Z."

"Don't blame me for answering you, Miss Masochist!"

"It's that bad?"

"Sacha is very discreet. He knows he's got to keep up an
image. Everybody's got an act in Hollywood. His is pretending
to be a dirty old producer. The truth is, he's been living with
Candice McIlhenney. Philadelphia Main Line McIlhenneys. Big
blue-blood bucks, baby."

"How long?" I asked, dragging the phone toward the
kitchen.

"Eleven years, my pet." I grab an open bottle of wine. "A
common-law couple. Candice rarely wants to go out. Prefers

the sedate life. Only surfaces at Sacha's insistence. Has a mind and a bank account of her own. She doesn't need him, which is how she keeps him. He sees other women. But for eleven years his heart has belonged to Candice. She accepts his philandering. . . . Stop crying! You asked! Certainly you didn't come to Hollywood to fall in love?"

"What's she look like?"

"Tall, thin, high forehead, elegant. A lady from Bryn Mawr. They all look the same, those dames. No T and A, sexpot!"

I had finished the wine. And the conversation. I took a Valium and passed out.

The next day I didn't go to the set. I told the director my ceiling had caved in due to the heavy rains.

The following day I had to await repairs.

For two days I stayed in bed with Jack Daniel's, Valium and MTV.

The weekend arrived. I decided to search the *L.A. Times*, *Hollywood Examiner*, *Variety*, *The Reporter* and every magazine covering Hollywood parties. I was looking for a photo of Candice McIlhenney.

On Sunday, I had a date with Sacha. I was nervous. I would confront him. No. I'd pop an Ecstasy and let the pill tell me what to do.

Sunday morning the phone rang. Long distance.

"Hello, this is Laurence."

My God, Jean-Paul's mother! How near she had come to being my mother-in-law! And I hadn't spoken to her for a year! She invited me to lunch on Wednesday. Of course, I could hardly see past my date with Sacha that night. I had no feelings left for Jean-Paul. I consulted myself. No. No feelings left.

Sacha took me to a tiny French restaurant for dinner. After ward we had sex as usual. Well, not quite as usual. He lost his erection in the middle of making love.

"You seem to be in a different space, Maya. Are you on something?"

I wanted to scream, "I'm on your fuckin' cock, you idiot!" but instead I dismounted him, curled up like a fetus and hugged a pillow. I knew he hated me on top. I had insisted. I felt like I was being sexy. I had to be sexy. What was wrong? He didn't care for me. That was it. He was thinking of Candice.

"Why do you take those pills?" Sacha asked. "You don't need them." He embraced me. "I want to be with *you*, not some chemical. You are beautiful. A wonder to make love to. And you give me such pleasure. Why do you take them?"

I began to cry. I remembered the first time I fell in love with pills. I was seventeen. I'd been having trouble sleeping. My father's bedsprings squeaked from his thrashing in the night until his pills—Thorazine, Miltown—knocked him out. My first boyfriend (he OD'd) told me about a Dr. Winston who'd give me pills for anything, but first I'd have to have a complete physical. Afterward a fatherly Dr. Winston said, "Miss Endicott, has anyone ever told you that you have a very small clitoris?"

That had been my problem all along! I felt different because I *was* different. So I had the foreskin of my clitoris cut away, as he suggested. One hour later while on a date with the Phys Ed teacher I hemorrhaged in a Howard Johnson's. Mom was furious, and told me never to see Dr. Winston again. But I kept going back to him for pills, especially Valium, and vitamin B-12 shots.

Not long afterward, with the help of a Quaalude, I had sex for the first time, with the Phys Ed teacher. It was great. Just like Dr. Winston said. Now my clit was the proper size. At least for a while. He told me it could grow back. African tribal women had these operations all the time to heighten their sensations. Now I had a new clitoris and pills and was ready for the world of men.

Sacha's erection returned. We ended the evening coming together. My pills worked wonders as usual.

The next night while leafing through *People* magazine at a Seven-11, I came upon a photo of Candice at a charity ball. Her brunette hair was slicked back into a chignon. She towered above a glowing Sacha. She was stunning. I bought the magazine and drove home in a daze.

Sacha never took me to parties. I met him at one, now I wasn't good enough to go to one with him. Was he hiding me from Candice? I felt like a once-a-week matinee. A fuck-and-run. His sexual gymnasium. What else was new?

When I walked into my apartment, I undressed, drew a bath and went to the kitchen to fix myself a rum and tonic. That would do it. Damn! No Bacardi. Thank God for liquor stores. They delivered.

Within five minutes there was a knock at the door. Carte Blanche knew I was a good customer. I looked through the peephole. A tall black man wearing a torn T-shirt and an apron stood holding a brown paper bag filled with hope.

I opened the door. "Just put it in the kitchen."

He said nothing. He seemed to know his way around. Had he been here before? I watched his lazy walk. Tight jeans covered an ample backside. High. Muscle-bound. Huge biceps bulged from under his stained T-shirt. He took direction well. I felt hot. Tingling. Buzzing. That damn buzzing. My armpits smelled. His black skin dripped with perspiration. His body odor left a trail. Mine followed. I liked that. I liked his silence.

"How much do I owe you?"

"Twenty-three sixty-five." His voice was low, rough, almost a growl. He had long black lashes and thick dark lips.

"Where did I put my handbag?" I said, fidgeting with the sash on my terrycloth robe. What next? I felt awkward. Helpless. I walked into the dining room and leaned over the table, looking for my wallet. My robe loosened. "Oh. It's in the bedroom. Sorry." I was always apologizing for myself. "It's OK," I said, walking up the stairs. "You can come up." He needed direction. Most men did.

My handbag was by the phone. As usual. I sat on the edge of the bed. A naked photo of me from modeling days hung on the far wall.

"That you, lady?" he asked, mesmerized.

I felt in competition with the photo, myself, the past. As I reached for my purse, my robe fell open. The buzzing was louder. Pressure filled my ears. Something was taking over. Possessing. My shyness vanished.

"Used to be," I said, reaching for my bag. My robe opened more. Not enough.

He stood a few feet away. Like a humble servant.

"Where's my checkbook? I can never find it when I need it," I said, scrounging around inside my bag.

My robe opened to my navel. My left breast was exposed. Pink flesh said hello to black. I looked into his eyes, magnets attracted to my nipples, then my belly button, then my blackness. I spread my legs, leaned back. The robe fell on the white satin bedspread.

He seemed to be in a trance too. It was like we were doing a strange dance. Our vibrations were music. His bald head glistened with sweat. He wore one earring.

"You like to watch?" I said, arching my back, stroking a nipple.

He wouldn't answer. Just stood there. His silence now lead.

I lay back on the bed. Posing. Modeling my wares, my goods, my merchandise. Advertising, promoting, selling.

"You like it?"

"What's not to like?" he said, unzipping his fly. Something fell out of his pocket.

"No," I said.

"Whaddaya mean, no?"

"I mean *no*. You can look, but you can't touch." I said it like a baby girl. Baby talk, that goddamn baby talk. I felt safe when I baby-talked in bed.

"Are you crazy, lady?"

We won't get into that, I thought. "Just watch," I said. "You'll like it. You'll see."

Now I was spread-eagled on the bed. Like in that screen test. Fingers rubbing between my legs. My fingers. My clitoris hardened. Like Dr. Winston said it should. Like producers, directors, cameramen wanted it to be. Like my mother forbade it to be. Sometimes I thought she had put a hex sign on my cunt. A spell. An evil spell.

I thought of Candice's photo, and my anger rubbed harder. Erasing. I pushed my pelvis up into his gaze. My juices felt pulled out of me, sucked across the room into his. His mouth opened. Saliva dripped on my gray wall-to-wall. I didn't care. Not like Harry Blydon. "Stain my carpet!" I wanted to shout. "Just don't stain me!"

I rubbed on. Harder. His eyes bulged. He stood spreading his legs, rotating his weight from side to side, arms crossed. I felt my spirit flow out and into his gaze. His energy devoured me. Without touching. Without words. Without offers. Without promises. My muscles tightened. My pelvis pushed upward. My pubic hair seemed to line his chin. I looked at his eyes. He didn't look at mine. He had other interests. He didn't want me either. What did I care? I was getting what I wanted. I was getting relief. I was getting back.

I heard a scream. My body collapsed. My anger dissolved. I felt soft. Serene. Good.

Then the shame.

I wanted him out.

The phone rang. Bless Pacific Telephone.

"Hello?" It was Z. "Can you hold on a minute?" The delivery man picked up the object he had dropped and stood there chewing gum.

I handed him the check as I put on my robe.

"One day, lady, you're gonna get yourself in real trouble."
Mumbling to himself he walked out the door.

Z had called to say some Arab friends were staying at the
Hollywood Hills Hotel. I should join them for cocktails. I did.
First I had a joint and walked Tutu. Then I studied Candice's
photo. Why? Again? What was wrong with me? I knew my
clitoris was wrong. So I had it corrected. But *I* couldn't be corrected. My mind—my deformity—couldn't be corrected. My
father tried to have his mind corrected. At least my operation
worked. When I touched myself and got hard, I knew it
worked. It wasn't a failure. I wasn't a failure. We weren't a
failure after all. I got that starring role because of my sexuality.
What I looked like. Thank God those producers, that director,
those studio heads didn't know what I felt like. A nothing. Bad.
Like Mom always said. I was wrong. And she was always right.

For the evening I wore a low-cut blouse as Z had suggested.
They were a crew of Saudi Arabians from Saint-Tropez—purple shirts, gold chains, champagne for *tout le monde*, caviar.

"Well, here's a toast to the star of *The Starlet*." Z held up her
glass. Henry Faisel held up a glass vial of cocaine that he had
heated with a blowtorch.

"Want a hit?" Henry asked.

"*Pourquoi pas?*" I said. I had never free-based. I inhaled.
Nothing happened. I inhaled again. Nothing. Exasperated, I
kept inhaling until I felt light-headed. After all, it was Friday
night. No shooting for two days. And I wanted to forget Candice and the photo of her that I had stuffed into my handbag.

Five hours later I found myself perched on a garbage can
outside Sacha's home, peering into his bedroom window. There
she was, in a champagne-colored negligee, quietly reading a
book in bed with Sacha, who was also reading a book. One hour
passed. They continued to read. Then Sacha turned off the light
on his side, kissed her on the cheek and fell asleep. She contin-

ued to read. I continued to watch. Half an hour later she pulled on black eyeshades and switched off her light.

I was furious. I wanted to watch them make love. Learn her secrets. Be convinced he didn't care for me. But she didn't seem to care about Sacha or sex.

My feet were swollen from standing on the garbage bin. I drove home.

The next morning I awoke without my mini, my blouse open, my shoes still on. When I walked Tutu, I noticed my car was parked in someone else's space. Car door open. My mini was in the back seat along with a man's black trousers, a gold Cartier watch and a purple shirt!

Oh dear!

On to lunch with Laurence.

THE restaurant would be La Maisonette. The owner was a friend of Jean-Paul's family. The French stick together like *crème brûlée*.

Laurence, a concert violinist, was a lady, a beautiful lady, beautiful as a queen. Her features haunted me sometimes. Yet her porcelain exterior could vanish with a smile. She was the mother every child dreamed of: vulnerable, but her heart was hidden from those she did not trust. Toward the world she could appear to be the Rock of Gibraltar.

Jean-Paul had heard the same tune—"Leave me alone. I must create. Go play!"—from both parents. He had, in a sense, been abandoned by Laurence as well as by Alessandro.

Now Laurence, who so valued her time, was taking me to lunch. Why? I was flattered. I simply loved looking at her. I was proud to be in her court.

Everything about her was wrong, yet she turned this inappropriateness into charm. She was long in the torso and short in the legs. She insisted on wearing bright colors. On holidays she wore red satin ribbons, silver sparkles, and sometimes she even put confetti in her hair. I wanted to dress her. I wanted to make Laurence as beautiful to others as she was to me. But as garish as her clothing might have been, when Laurence walked into a room all eyes focused on her. The people stuffing their mouths this Wednesday afternoon were no exception.

She was wearing a printed jacket over a clashing print dress.

She smiled, happy to see me. She kissed both my cheeks. I hoped she didn't smell my hangover.

"Good to see you, Maya. You're looking lovely as ever."

I returned the compliment.

She sat erect, her hands clasped in her lap. I remembered asking her how she was able to sit so straight and walk so tall.

She'd giggled. "I imagine I'm carrying a firm grapefruit between my buttocks. And I squeeze."

Her piercing green, almond-shaped eyes stared into mine. She was one of those upper-class French ladies who come to the point quickly. "Jean-Paul and I drove through Switzerland this winter. We were able to talk. How private he can be at times." Her eyes held mine. "You are the only woman he has ever loved."

I was—to my surprise—numb. "What happened to little old Vivien Leigh?" Vivien Leigh was the name I had given a model who had moved in after me.

"Over . . . long ago. Jean-Paul's on his way here from India, and he will call you. I know. Maya, stop this foolishness. Get married. I want to help."

I couldn't believe my ears. I had always thought Laurence hated me, and though I looked up to her, I was afraid of her, her need to control. (She reminded me of me.) She had legally arranged for Jean-Paul to have his father's last name, though an opposing Alessandro had said, "My name is a curse. Anyone who takes my name will lose his identity."

The year after Laurence left the Nobel Prize–winning Alessandro, it was rumored that she married Dr. Maurice Goldschmidt, the latest Nobel Prize recipient to prove to Alessandro she was genius-worthy—that a genius would marry her. (It takes a star-fucker to know a genius-fucker.) But before she consented to marry M. Goldschmidt, she demanded he sign a pussy-whipping prenuptial agreement granting her the right to live anywhere for three months each year—alone. Play around she did. Jean-Paul and I met her lovers.

M. Goldschmidt, a fellow star-fucker, was thrilled to marry

Alessandro's ex under any conditions, thereby gaining entrée into a society to which a Jewish boy born in Newark would not be privy—no matter how many magazine covers his intellectual face graced.

I never met Dr. Goldschmidt. To me he was only someone who paid for Laurence's expensive tastes. The irony was that Laurence claimed she left Alessandro because of his infidelity. The French pot was calling the Italian kettle black.

Despite Laurence's manipulations, I understood her and respected her courage, her outrageousness. Now I had to force myself to confront her, to tell her the truth.

"Laurence, I've never been able to talk to you," I said to her now. "When I broke up with Jean-Paul, I said to him, 'You are doing to me what your father did to your mother.'"

She made a sound at this. She sucked in her breath. She looked about to cry.

The maître d' brought us champagne—on the house. We got a little drunk to celebrate. We wept when we said goodbye.

While waiting for the valet to deliver my car, I waved to my agent, who had just arrived. He was with a man who looked familiar. A black man. Probably one of his tricks. The black man stared, waved at me, then whispered to my agent. It was the delivery man, the Carte Blanche liquor man.

I began to tremble. Driving was difficult. I felt light-headed, dizzy. When I walked into the apartment I went to the liquor cabinet, mixed a martini and called Sacha. He would make it better. What could one bald black guy do? No one would believe him. Would they?

Sacha was free. We began making love the minute he walked through the door. All the while, I thought of that delivery man.

April 10. A note was under my door. "Be calling you in three weeks to collect $20,000—cash. Unless you want Hollywood to know about your flashing clit. Especially your agent. Your voice sounds real sexy on tape."

● ● ●

Jean-Paul was due in three weeks. I'd have to get the money somehow. How had he taped my voice? Then I remembered that he had dropped something. A mini recorder?

No one must know. Not even Z. I popped two Quaaludes, drank a pint of scotch and passed out.

The next morning I called Carte Blanche. The bald black man had quit.

I telephoned my agent, Michael.

"He wouldn't tell me his name," Michael said. "I met him when I ordered a case of bourbon. He said to call him Mr. Carte Blanche. Leather queens are slippery, Maya. I couldn't resist showing off my latest delivery to those motherstuffers at La Maisonette. My dear, men and women were drooling on their endive. Obviously you too. That why the Q and A?"

I dodged the response and hung up.

April 13. I had only a week left on *The Starlet*. I couldn't wait. Jean-Paul called. "Where are you?" I asked. I wanted him. That moment. In my arms.

"New Delhi." He sounded like he was smiling.

"You get around."

"I heard about your lunch." Then he laughed. "Laurence is still up to her old tricks."

"I never knew she liked me."

"That's been your tune for years, dearie."

"Are you coming to L.A.?"

"In three weeks." (That's too late! I thought.)

"Tutu and I will be waiting at the airport."

"Want anything from the Indians?"

"A sari."

"Still *mon petit bébé?*"

"What do you think?"

"Keep the boutique open." (When we made love, Jean-Paul

would say he was opening my boutique. By that measure, Sacha had opened my department store and a couple of branches.)

"Watch your shopping. Don't spend it all."

I hung up and cuddled Tutu and told him his master was coming home. He gave a loud cry, nearly human. One more poodle trying to talk.

Damn, he wouldn't be coming for three more weeks! I would have to get the money from Sacha. Before we made love, he would leave his wallet on the dresser. When he was in the bathroom I would go through it, looking for photos of Candice. He always had a few blank checks. What if Sacha found out? That was the risk. In art class I had gotten an A in calligraphy. I could do it.

So what if he found out. I would charm him. Treat him like I did Harry Blydon. I was afraid. Carte Blanche could ruin me in Hollywood. Ruin me with Jean-Paul. Ruin me, period. I would have to use Sacha as I felt he was using me. These thoughts and a pitcher of martinis seemed to be the solution.

Three days later I saw Sacha and pulled it off. I liked doing it because it was getting back. Getting back for all those parties he never invited me to, getting back for his not leaving Candice, getting back for his once-a-week fuck-and-run.

Cashing the check was another matter.

I called Alvin, my friend at the Bank of America. (Sacha used Security Pacific.) I plugged one end of a bugging device into my Sony tape recorder and attached the suction cup at the other end to the outside part of the telephone that pressed against my ear.

"Alvin, sorry to bother you, but a friend of mine is writing a screenplay and wants to know how a character would cash a forged check for a large amount."

"All you need, Maya, is some secret info on the guy, like his mother's maiden name, his date and place of birth and Social Security number. Have your character act snotty, be in a hurry, intimidate. If the bank's client is wealthy, no one at his branch will know what he looks like."

My tape jammed. One of those cheap Radio Shack cassettes. Damn! I banged the recorder.

"Oh," Alvin said, "And have the guy cash the check at lunch. Officers are out. Poor bank employee gets fired. That's that!"

Sam, the film's wardrobe man, would do anything for me. I was going to find out just how much. The next day just before lunch I approached Sam on the set.

"I can't explain it, Sam, but would you cash a check posing as your least favorite producer . . . Sacha Shactel?"

He hesitated.

"Thought you'd do anything for me, Sam?" I said, tweaking his beard.

"What do I get out of it?"

"Want a piece of the action?"

"Yep. But not money."

Sam and I adjourned to my trailer, where I gave him what I had given Harry Blydon and all the rest.

The following night, dressed in a three-piece suit, looking exactly like Sacha, Sam, who had shaved his beard, arrived at my apartment holding a brown paper bag filled with $20,000.

"Hope this solves your problems, Maya."

I thanked him. He didn't leave. He wanted more, he wanted sex whenever he was in the mood. I took two Quaaludes. What had I created?

Mr. Carte Blanche called exactly on schedule. I met him at the corner Arco station and gave him the brown paper bag filled with Sacha's money. He had long ropelike hair, dreadlocks. A Rastafarian wig. His growl remained the same. "Hope this is all of it, lady. If it isn't, I'll get back to you." He threw me the cassette, then peeled the rubber of the tires of a brand-new silver Porsche. A dealer, I thought. He had to be a dope dealer.

I would have to leave town. Permanently. Thank God Jean-Paul was coming.

At Sun Bee Liquors I bought a fifth of Jack Daniel's. I drove home in a rage, finished the fifth, then passed out.

The next morning, hung over again, I popped an Alka-Seltzer and Valium, the perfect combo. Jean-Paul was due in on Air India at 6 P.M.

As I cleaned the apartment I thought, What does Jean-Paul want from me? Or, more precisely, what do I want from Jean-Paul? I wanted to get away from Hollywood. I felt old at thirty-three, too old to be discovered. No one would hire me after this film. Each morning I would look into the mirror, see new lines, new crow's-feet. I was tired of the mirror, tired of watching gravity reconstruct my face. I didn't yet need a facelift or those clamps and tape older actresses used when filming to pull up loose flesh and hide it somewhere behind the ears, but I could see how useful these devices were. My lighting in the film was the pits. I could feel it. My agent had warned me. I had wanted to quit *The Starlet*. Not because I didn't like acting. Acting was fun. It got me in touch with my feelings. I was able to do things in front of a camera that I was unable to do in life. That felt good, daring, bold. In reality I was oversensitive, inhibited; I had to push myself to be assertive.

In a way flashing was like acting; the trancelike state that overtook my body was like a character overcoming deep repression. Playing roles with exaggerated sexuality was perfect for my stuffed-up, bottled-up feelings that never felt the right to surface without society's permission.

No, I wanted to quit *The Starlet* because I had seen three days of rushes and couldn't bear the way I looked. Better quit Hollywood before it quits me. Getting married would solve the problem, or so my mother said.

But whom would I marry? Better yet, who would marry me? I would marry whoever asked me, but I preferred Sacha to Jean-Paul. Maybe I could use Jean-Paul's interest to make Sacha jealous? Yep, a proposal from Jean-Paul would force Sacha's hand. It was six months since we had seen each other, and I still felt something for him, despite my love for Sacha. I was going to try to think of the good times, try to fall in love with him all over again.

About three o'clock Tutu and I began dressing. I brushed his hair and mine. I wore the bright blue silk pantsuit Jean-Paul had given me the previous summer. Tutu wore a typed message taped to his collar: "Welcome home."

We jumped into the Fiat and sped down La Cienega Boulevard toward the airport. Jean-Paul was coming home, if only for a short time. Maybe walking out on him had been the right thing to do. After all, that's what his mother had done to his father, and he loved his mother more than any other woman; therefore the woman most like Laurence he would love the most. I hoped.

"Think of the good times," I said to Supertoots as we drove by the Beverly Center. "When he took care of us. When he played his harmonica and wrote songs about us. When he took us for walks and did our dishes and our laundry and cooked for us. Remember? *Gigot*." Tutu whined. "*Pot-au-feu*." Tutu barked. "*Lapin au forestier*." Tutu drooled.

"We must remember the good times," I said as we passed oil fields covered with those mechanical geese with long metal necks bobbing up and down looking for something that might or might not be there.

"How about that birthday party we gave him and you signed the cake with your paw? Then you and I danced with him. And he held us. We must remember the good times," I said as we drove into the airport parking lot. Tutu barked and barked.

His plane had landed.

There he was. His brown shoulder-length hair had been cut. He was wearing the monogrammed Brooks Brothers shirt I had bought him the year before, a three-piece suit and a tie. He looked like a businessman. A beautiful businessman. Except for the tell-tale harmonica jutting out of his breast pocket. He hadn't spotted me, but Tutu got a whiff of him and his stub of a tail began to wag. He cried, pulled, scratched at the Astroturf carpet.

Jean-Paul spotted me. Gave a smile. That smile. He was still handsome, still my kinda guy.

He dropped his briefcase, put his arms around me and held me. Tutu pulled at his cuffs. Jean-Paul held him too. We three embraced. Our family was reunited, if only for the moment. Why had I ever left?

Maybe I had acted impetuously. Had I really given Jean-Paul a chance to adjust from pauper to millionaire? I had given him an ultimatum: "Give me a date for the wedding or I'm not re-turning to Paris after my father's funeral."

No matter how earnest my reason for leaving him, it was still pressure—pressure on a childlike Jean-Paul who was trying to grow up just as I was. Pressure on an emotionally immature man who had both loved and hated his own father. He had been abandoned by Alessandro and was confused with his new role in life, which he viewed as replacing Alessandro. But now his position and his megamillions had given him a larger, more sturdy set of balls. I couldn't play *rompe balle* (Italian for ball-breaking) as I had in the past.

He was still wearing Guerlain's Habit Rouge. I loved the scent. I loved Jean-Paul. I thought about Sacha. How different they were. But both were stubborn. Somehow that comforted me.

Tutu couldn't stop wiggling. Now he peed on Jean-Paul's foot. Calculated poodle hysteria. Jean-Paul didn't scold but tapped Tutu on his *tête*. "Hey, hey, Monsieur Supertoots. *Ça va pas, non?*"

Tutu laughed. His upper lip went up and his gorgeous incisors showed.

"You haven't changed," I said.

"Are you kidding? Look at my hair. I want a transplant."

"I want a facelift."

"*Bébé!* You could use a mind lift."

"Lobotomies run in the family."

"I love you the way you are."

We picked up his bags, returned to my apartment, put Tutu in his *salle de bain* and set up the boutique. He was the shop-keeper. I was the shop. Each night he'd open me. Some days we took inventory. Other days we interviewed help. Or installed new merchandise. Or had a fire sale. Tonight we had a rummage sale and fired angry employees left over from the past. Best of all, I forgot about the delivery man.

Jean-Paul touched me like no other man. I felt like the finest, most delicate pastry in his arms. He would hold me as a baby holds its first toy. His fingertips were special, filled with energy. Transmitters of his mind. He always made me feel he'd take care of me. Never leave me. Never abandon me. Make me whole.

His legs were long, like his father's. He wrapped them around me tight and pushed himself inside. His movements were clear.

Clean. Forceful. And controlled. He had dark brown pubic hair. Straight and long. I liked to comb it. Stroke it. Play with it. Braid it. But mostly admire it. He squeezed his legs, aimed high. A straight shooter all the way.

I loved his sexy body. All muscles. Not a bulge. I would kiss his skin for hours. Everywhere. I would look for blackheads. He would look for mine. I would remove them. He would remove mine. I would give him manicures. Pedicures. Shampoo his head. Massage his scalp like his mother did. He liked that. He liked baths together. Long baths. We'd hug. Play around like two kids, happy to be home.

He was the first man I ever loved. We had met when I was twenty-six. I had never felt such magnetism, such a need for someone. Now, I loved Sacha too. Sacha could be Jean-Paul's father. Or mine. The three of us could be a family. I could have sex with both of them at the same time. That's what I wanted, both of them. But Sacha wasn't interested. Jean-Paul was. He was younger than I by four years. I wouldn't mess up this time. Not like the last time. I would do as he said. Be smart. Not push him around. Until he said "I do." Then I'd let him have it. PAFF! Then I could see Sacha. And have money for plane fare.

These thoughts (all too many of them) went through my head as we made love. My mind exhausted me. My body was his. My bed was his. My cunt was his. My mind wasn't. I stopped thinking. Let him push me around. Control me! Do it to me! Spaces opened up. I felt high. Light. Free. Loved. I cried. Jean-Paul moaned. Tutu barked. My mind shut off. Finally at rest, we all fell asleep.

I had fallen in love with Jean-Paul all over again, just as I had hoped I would. He was my way out.

The next morning he brought me breakfast. We liked to eat in bed. Dinner. Lunch. Each other. We gave lie-down candlelit dinners for two.

•   •   •

"I read that you starred in a movie."

"Hopefully my last." I lied. Though I was unhappy with the filming of *The Starlet*, I wanted the option of returning to acting. I wanted my life to be mine. But now I had to let Jean-Paul think my life was his.

"Stubborn little Capricorn," Jean-Paul said to me.

I turned on the radio. It was the first thing I did in the morning: rock 'n' roll and coffee. The Police screamed, "The DOO DOO DOO and the DA DA DA."

"Whatever happened to Vivien Leigh?" I asked him.

"I caught on to her act. She tried to get pregnant. I threw her out." He gave a Gallic shrug. "Guess what I have for my little chickadee?"

"A sari?"

"Da-DA!" After this fanfare, he held up a saffron polyester sari. A polyester sari? I'd never seen a polyester sari. I couldn't believe it. He hadn't changed. He was still cheap, like his father. But I had to accept him, rather than try to change him. At least for now.

He held it, waiting for me to put it on. I turned my back as I slipped into it, relieved he couldn't see my expression.

As I was getting ready to bubble with false pleasure, I felt an object in the pocket. A piece of jewelry. A ring. The antique engagement ring I thought he'd given Vivien Leigh.

He was grinning and a tear fell from his eye. "Wanna get married in Vegas, *bébé?*"

My tears fell on the robe. I was glad it was polyester. I had to marry him.

"Well, whaddaya say?"

"I do . . . but not in Vegas." We had to be married somewhere far away—in Europe.

We reopened the boutique.

Later, we discussed wedding plans. I used the excuse that I wanted it to be in Paris because, after all, it was his hometown. He believed me. Besides, now that he was in megafrancs I wanted to spend it. Wedding reception at the Tour d'Argent. Fly in all my friends and serve pressed duck for the chosen.

Au revoir, Hollywood. I would be his wife. I'd learn to love the Paris I hated, learn to love the rain and French TV. I'd learn to love Jean-Paul all over again.

So we agreed to have the wedding in Paris. I would fly over in three weeks. Jean-Paul left two days later to meet with his bankers.

I called Z. Maybe her big mouth would give Sacha those details I didn't have the courage to provide.

"Well, big buns," said Z, "how's the love affair?"

"Which one?"

"What do you mean? Your Russian stud, dearie."

"Oh, him."

"Got another in the broom closet?"

"Jean-Paul just left."

"When'd he get here?"

"In and out. He loves me."

"Ooh la la! Your irons are *très chaud!"*

"I don't know what to do with Sacha."

"What makes you think you got to do anything? Enjoy him. That's what I do with Johnny Jordan and the rest."

"Why stay married, Z?"

"Fringe benefits, dearie. I eat my cake and I eat others too."

"Well, Jean-Paul wants to marry me."

"Lordy."

"What should I do?"

"Start thinking. Read Harold Robbins."

"I hate reading. I can't concentrate."

"Harold Robbins isn't reading. He's a psychologist. Play one against the other. That's his theory. And you got nice loaded dice. Roll 'em."

"I think I love them both. What if I try to use Jean-Paul's proposal to get Sacha to marry me?"

"Good game plan! Hey, Ms. Torn-Between, marrying Jean-Paul wouldn't be that bad. I'd go for the bucks and forget the bullshit. On that financial note, I'm hangin'."

Click.

Money wasn't going to be the deciding factor.

No, I loved Sacha more than Jean-Paul because he accepted me as I was—an actress and a flasher. He understood my shame and gave me confidence I could overcome this sexual addiction. "Your mother sexually abused you by forcing enemas upon you," he said. "Had your mother ever been sexually abused by her parents?" (Fat chance I'd ever get the Pennsylvania Dutch to cop to incest.)

Lord knows how Jean-Paul would react if he knew about the delivery man and cab driver and the rest of them.

Sacha and I had a date a few days later. He told me about the missing check and the $20,000. My surprise would have won me an Oscar. Nevertheless, I felt real love from him. Although he wouldn't say the words, his actions showed it. So I didn't need to hear it. Not completely, but I did need to tell him about Jean-Paul.

The words spouted out. "Sacha, I'm moving to Paris. I'm getting married."

"When did all this come about?"

"Last week."

"But you never spoke of anyone else."

"Neither did you."

"I assumed you knew about Candice."

"I only found out two weeks ago."

"We're just good friends. We've been together eleven years."

My heart landed in a dull place when he said that. Now I knew how much Sacha valued his position in the community and his reputation and his bank account and his invitations to fine parties. It all revolved around Candice. Sacha was passionate in bed, but not out. He wasn't about to pick up my bat and hit a home run for me or anyone who might jeopardize his holdings.

I was glad I'd stolen his money. I was glad I had made Sacha pay. He probably would have given me the money. He understood my flashing, but I wanted to hurt Sacha anyway. Nevertheless, I still loved him, was obsessed by him.

If I married Jean-Paul, maybe Sacha would respect me.

But I didn't respect Jean-Paul. He could never "get his shit together," one of his favorite expressions. I was in awe of the power of creativity, the glamour of accomplishment. Jean-Paul couldn't keep a job. He had tried writing, directing, painting—and got precisely nowhere.

Sacha had produced five Oscar-winning films.

Jean-Paul was just like that cab driver—a follower. There was one essential difference—he had $70 million.

But accumulation of wealth didn't turn me on. Fame did.

Jean-Paul lacked ambition, the courage to take a risk. Risk-taking was another sexy kind of power. Each film project was a risk to Sacha.

Jean-Paul was not motivated by self. He was motivated by Alessandro's fame. I didn't mind this when Jean-Paul needed me. I wanted to be needed. I liked that control. But his new wealth had freed him. Jean-Paul had outgrown me. And I had outgrown him.

I was no longer content with a copy of his father.

I wanted the real thing. To make love to fame . . . Sacha.

But if I married Jean-Paul, I would be famous. Fame rubs off. Hollywood had shown me that stars are the biggest star-fuckers of us all. Fame marries fame. I wanted something to offer Sacha's weaknesses. And mine as well.

IT would be a June wedding. *Grand-mère* Grinda's garden in her ivory-white carriage house on Avenue Foch would be in bloom. Jean-Paul had nixed the Tour d'Argent. I wasn't about to hassle him—yet. On came the guest lists. Food. Music. Transportation. Hotels. Honeymoon. I felt like I was giving a big party for myself, and it felt good. Thoughts of Sacha were buried under my wedding plans.

Since our apartment near the Invalides was being renovated, we were staying with *grand-mère*. While I was closing my apartment in Hollywood, saying goodbye to Sacha and trying to hide my whereabouts to-be, Jean-Paul had been ordering new furniture. Even an all-aluminum German-made kitchen. Everything was changed. No memories of the past. "This time we're gonna make it," he said when he met Tutu and me at the airport. He had bought us presents for Paris's inclement weather—a silver raincoat for Tutu and a silver Bentley for me. The money from the estate had been coming in. In buckets! The polyester sari had been a gag.

Alessandro had loved gags.

For the wedding *grand-mère* was finally going to take the plastic off her living room furniture.

I couldn't believe it. I remembered peeking into the salon (the door was always closed) and seeing the sofa, chairs, lamps, and carpet covered in plastic bags of the sort you use for sweaters. Mausoleum Manor.

But when she taught me French, I forgave her strange ways. Each day I would go to Fauchon, buy six or seven *pâtisseries* and bring them back to *grand-mère's salle à manger* with its poker-green walls, one table, four chairs and a French window. She didn't speak English. I sort of spoke French. What Jean-Paul called *caniche française* (French for dogs). She would give me a French lesson over *les gâteaux avec du thé* underneath the portrait of Laurence by Matisse, a friend of the family. I loved *grand-mère*. She was short, burly, and wore sponge-soled walking shoes and the same gray skirt and lavender cardigan over a white blouse seven days in a row. Yet her closets were filled.

She had a high laugh that would cause her to shake and hold her sides like Santa Claus. She wore subtle makeup. Her brows were penciled in and her hair dyed black, but she never plucked her slight moustache. That I liked too. It was all part of *grand-mère*.

Jean-Paul said she was on the dykey side like my mother. I told him I liked *grand-mère* because she was *grand-mère*.

Supertoots loved her. Super T. He had the run of the maisonette at 18, Avenue Foch.

He was even part of the house band. Once each month, on a Sunday afternoon, the family got together for a jam session in the *salle à manger*. Jean-Paul would move the tables and chairs aside and then he'd pull out his harmonica. Laurence would play her violin, Grams would play her clarinet, Chanda played the piano and sang (usually trying to imitate Marlene Dietrich —much to the rest of the band's dismay). I'd tie bells to Tutu's collar, which would ring with his frenzied attempts to remove them, often in rhythm. When he was in town, it was rumored, Maurice Goldschmidt would play drums. "A family who plays together stays together," was Laurence's motto.

Today Laurence was going to buy me a wedding gown. Chanda and Laurence and I were off to Pierre La Roche to select the dress from his summer collection. Chanda, after her great success with her purple toilet seat, was dabbling in decorating

and, with all her lately arrived megafrancs, had become the darling of the decorating world. Everyone wanted to be near Alessandro. If they couldn't touch him, the daughter would
certainly do. Chanda used this to her advantage. I always kept
one eye focused on all six feet of Chanda, who was jealous of
Jean-Paul's affection for me. She had introduced him to that
model, Vivien Leigh.

Chanda was treacherous. She had inherited her mother's craf-
tiness and her father's talent and bizarre sense of humor, but no
one's looks. She looked like a Brueghel painting of an Italian or a
Botero drawing of a chubby-cheeked child grown up. From a
distance she resembled a truck driver on the Appian Way. Im-
mense, sturdy, flat-chested. Not fat, but pudgy. Her face had
the handsomeness of a bullfighter going in for the kill. Because
she had tremendous style, on some days she managed to turn
her masculine appearance into a dignified beauty. Chanda had
been born with a speech impediment. Although she spoke five
languages, this didn't help her impediment. She was taking
speech lessons, had been for two years. I would hear her shouting her exercises all over the carriage house. Sometimes I felt
sorry for her and respected her courage. Especially when, overcoming her speech impediment, she developed an involuntary
twitch in her eyes. Knitting seemed to help her eye muscles to
relax. Everywhere Chanda went, her knitting needles were sure
to go. Jean-Paul and his harmonica, Chanda and her needles.

Each season she dyed her hair a new color. For the summer
wedding it would be purple.

Jean-Paul moved like a clown. Laurence wore colored ribbons
like a clown. Chanda looked like a clown.

When I was with "the family" I felt like I was at a three-ring
circus waiting for one of them to perform, to do his or her act to
get attention. I felt like their audience. I was.

Two years ago a completely naked Chanda starred in a Swed-
ish art film, much to the family's disgrace. Chanda's black bush
of a pussy flashed all over continental Europe. I guess I wasn't

the only flasher in the family. I knew she did it to shove a wad at her father, who was still alive then and had refused to see not only Jean-Paul, but also Chanda and Laurence, for the past fifteen years.

We three women met in the lobby of the building in which Monsieur P. La Roche had his salon. P. La Roche was France's top designer and Chanda's confidant. Laurence, Chanda and I crowded into a small *ascenseur* with black wrought-iron gates that closed behind us with a clank. I could feel Chanda breathing down my neck. Laurence silently stared at the ceiling. At the third floor, the elevator landed with a thud. Chanda blinked and said, "Ooi!" opening the gates in one fell swoop.

The woman who opened the door of the salon had her hair pulled back tightly into a bun and wore a well-tailored suit. She smiled as though she were Japanese and offered us seats as though they were cups of tea. The all-white foyer was lacquered to a heavy shine. The Breuer cane chairs were not imitations. After a few minutes an apparently shy, myopic—he wore thick horn-rimmed glasses—P. La Roche slipped into the room. Quietly he introduced himself. No gushing. No sales pitch. No phony compliments. Tall, bone-thin and blond, he wore a beige, impeccably tailored three-piece suit and reminded me of a younger, well-dressed Andy Warhol. *"Bonjour,"* he said softly, shaking our hands gently. He kissed Chanda, now sporting bullfrog-green hair, on both cheeks, *à la Française.*

Chanda said, bubbling and blinking, "Pierre, Pierre, I have new designs for the *salle à manger."*

"Merci, Chanda, a little later, *non?* I am in love with your hair. What a marvelous Lautrec green. Why, you must be approaching your Fauve period. Ah, but today we want a wedding dress for the lovely Maya, *n'est-ce pas? Suivez-moi, s'il vous plaît."*

Chanda scampered after him like a hungry child following the Good Humor man. I went next—the middle woman. Laurence wanted to be last. She wanted to be coaxed.

The back of the salon was chaos. Seamstresses were sewing

and cutting. Long wooden tables were strewn with fabric. Sewing machines were humming loudly. Neon lights covered all. Dresses hung on racks, on dummies; his latest samples hung on hangers suspended from the ceiling.

P. La Roche pointed to one long eggshell satin gown with tiny beads trimming the bodice, the sleeves and the small train. It was magnificent. "Bianca Jagger bought this as well. Madame, would your beautiful daughter-in-law like to try it on?" A clever P. La Roche was now directing all his attention to Laurence, who was paying the bill.

"What do you think of it, Maya? After all, it is your dress."

How silly three women are together. P. La Roche must have been laughing inside. Designers know women so well.

Suddenly P. La Roche snapped his fingers. The woman in the gray suit with the Japanese smile instantly appeared holding the same dress. "You must be a size eight," P. La Roche said, adjusting the rim of his glasses. "The dressing room is behind that curtain." He pointed to a corner of the room.

Chanda, who had been eyeing the samples with envy, blinking more furiously than ever, said, "Can I try on that fabulous maroon skirt? The fabric is so unusual." She wiggled her behind enthusiastically in her loose beige linen pleated slacks.

"*Mais bien sûr.* You can use the same *cabinet* as Maya if it's all right with her."

I couldn't object but, boy, did I want to. I turned my back to Chanda as I took off my bra, and faced right smack into a full-length mirror. Chanda's eyes were focused on my naked breasts, then traveled down my body much like a man's might—calculated and mean. Slowly she unzipped her fly and removed her slacks. I didn't look at her.

Quickly I slipped the dress over my head and asked her to do up the back. She looked at me as though she were taking my corpuscle count. Her hands touched my body in a too familiar way. By the time she finished buttoning it felt like the year 2000.

I practically ran back to Laurence to model the gown. I had a quick look in the mirror and said I loved it. Any dress would have done. I wanted to get out of there tootie sweetie.

After a few *ooh la la*'s from P. La Roche and Laurence and silence from Chanda, we split.

I wondered if someone—maybe a man—had given Chanda enemas against her will. Her anger had invaded her marrow, built up since Alessandro had abandoned her. Her life could be one vindictive flow of energy. How wonderful that she was talented and could create rather than vegetate in her angry shell. I wished I had Chanda's talent. I would have liked her to be my friend. But she wouldn't let me get close to her. Anyone who understood her pain and wanted an intimate friendship threatened her. Chanda was part of *la vie mondaine*, as Grams used to say, which protected her from ever having to get close to anyone who could hurt her. Superficial friends and a superficial lifestyle represented a safe refuge. Chanda, Laurence and Jean-Paul still loved Alessandro. But how could they not be angry with him? He was the joker in the deck of dads.

With Jean-Paul looking more like his father the older he became, Laurence and Chanda now transferred their love of Alessandro to Jean-Paul. Jean-Paul played into their affections because they made him feel wanted and he could get back at Alessandro if his own mother and Alessandro's daughter fancied him sexually. They're French, I kept telling myself. They're just being French.

Back on Avenue Foch I showed Grams my wedding dress-to-be.

"Look, *grand-mère, c'est joli, n'est-ce pas?*"

"Very, very prittee!" (I was teaching Grams English.)

The dress reminded me of something Candice would have chosen. I wondered if I could invite Sacha to the wedding. Why not? And Candice. We could all be friends. French friends.

I decided to send the invitation. Maybe Sacha would surprise me. If not, he would at least know how to reach me.

Then I thought I'd call Z.

"Well, sexpot, how's your frog?"

"*Ça va* so far. Got my wedding dress yesterday."

"Some piece of work, I'll bet."

"Good enough for Candice."

"Still stuck on the stud?" asked Z.

"Only as a fringe benefit, like you taught me."

"Herr Fringe Benefit seems pretty beat up these days. Methinks he misses you."

"Serves the Cossack right."

"Ain't you gotten tough? Is it the croissants?"

"I'm reading Harold Robbins. My sex life needn't end with marriage, right?"

"That's the spirit, barf bag."

"So let's have lunch."

"You expect me to hop on the Concorde for lunch?"

"Come over three weeks before the wedding. Stay at our flat by the Invalides."

"We'll pop up after the Cannes Film Festival."

"Maybe you'll see Sacha."

"Could be. He always seems to show up."

"Bring him with you."

"If you give me ten percent of Jean-Paul's bucks after you get your alimony."

"Not so quick. I may never get divorced. Like you."

"Camp follower."

"Z, you just keep manicuring Eric's feet."

"*Ciao.*"

Hurrah. Z would bring the action. Some action! I ran downstairs to open a bottle of wine. Jean-Paul was coming in. A dullness covered his eyes. He seemed lost, confused, tired from confrontations with lawyers and excessive talk about his father.

"Alessandro was not together," he would say. "He was a child. A fucking baby child. And my problem is trying to be better than him, not as a writer, but as a person. I'm trying to repair myself and all my tracks. People who knew his work thought 'Whew! Terrific!' They didn't know the man. His biggest failing was himself, his development of self."

When Jean-Paul talked about his father, was he talking about himself? Was all the inventorying of Alessandro's possessions a way for Jean-Paul to communicate with his father?

Tonight Jean-Paul looked sad.

"How was your day?" I asked.

"Boring bankers. Red tape." He kissed me on the cheeks. "But the b-bucks keep on with the flow."

I held up the bottle of wine. "Want a glass?"

"Of course. Chanda here?" As soon as Jean-Paul returned at the end of the day, he would seek out Chanda.

"In her room."

"We'll have it there."

Chanda, wearing a red sweater, pillbox hat with a red feather, red high heels and see-through pantyhose, was knitting, as usual.

"How were the lawyers?" she asked, blinking as she faced Jean-Paul and adjusted the crotch of her pantyhose.

Jean-Paul didn't have any reaction. My temperature was rising.

"*Vino?*" Jean-Paul asked.

"You know I never drink before a date."

"Ah, Madame has a date. Which of your fine faggot friends?"

"I don't find that so amusing. Maybe if you were nicer to a few people, you'd be invited by Jasper and Curtis more often." Chanda waved her knitting needles in the air.

"I'd rather read Céline."

"Then read him, but keep your comments about my friends to yourself."

Chanda sat at the dressing table with her legs spread and began doing her eye makeup. She had to concentrate not to blink to put on mascara. Perspiration dripped from my armpits.

"Jean-Paul, let's leave Chanda alone."

"No, darling, I love company," Chanda said.

I grabbed Jean-Paul's hand and the wine bottle and ushered him out of her emerald-green and purple boudoir. She had painted it. The loo matched. The famous toilet seat, purple. Its lid, green. A disaster area. Too many art classes at the Beaux-Arts had made Chanda dangerous with a paintbrush.

Once I closed the door to our bedroom, I felt safe. Its ceiling, of painted azure skies and cumulus clouds, was refreshing.

"Don't you feel uncomfortable around your sister," I asked, "with her pussy hanging out like that?"

"I've gotten used to it." (He meant "I enjoy every minute of it!")

"Why don't you say something?"

"Don't make this an *histoire*. It's simple. Chanda likes me because I look like my father. So does Laurence."

I didn't answer. Instead I undressed and got into bed. But I was thinking of the time Laurence drove the family to Brittany. Because of her bad back, she had insisted Jean-Paul sit next to her in the front of their Daimler, while I was put in the back next to Chanda.

At dinner that night Laurence toasted Jean-Paul, and looked into his eyes like she was giving head. I thought Jean-Paul enjoyed those moments too.

That night the boutique was *fermée*. I dreamed of Sacha.

In the morning I called my mother. Never a lot of fun there.

"How's it going, Mom? Almost packed?"

"What else do I have to do?"

"Paris will be fun."

"Not at my age. You could have had the wedding right here in Philadelphia."

We kept it going back and forth from Philadelphia to Paris to Philadelphia until we hung up.

The wedding was closing in.

• • •

The morning before the wedding Jean-Paul served me breakfast in bed. As I buttered my croissant, he pulled a paper out of his briefcase. "Please be understanding, Maya. The estate's lawyers have draw up this prenuptial agreement. It's merely a f-formality," he said with wide-eyed innocence as his voice seemed to rise an octave and crack. Then he grinned as if he had just told a bad joke.

I glanced at the lengthy legal document. "What is it?"

"In the event of divorce my father's estate must be left intact."

"What?"

"It was not my idea," he said, lowering his voice.

The papers clearly stated that in the event of divorce I was entitled to zilch. *Nada!* Nothing!

"How can you? Where's your trust?" I said, throwing the papers at him.

"That's the way the lawyers say it has to be. Don't make a big deal out of it. Unless you are m-marrying me for my money."

Further arguing and tears got me nowhere. He wanted my life to be his. To keep control of me by giving me an allowance, limitations, rules. He was letting me know that marrying him would still not make me part of his family. Avarice bound this family—money. That was the green blood that made everyone slightly mad, jealous, vindictive. No wonder Alessandro had cut himself off from them. Why did I want to be part of this insanity and greed?

The Starlet had been a joke. I was too old to continue the charade—pretending I was being discovered at age thirty-three. Sacha didn't want to claim me. He worshiped the same green blood. Marrying me didn't give anyone any power, financial gain or prestige. Marriage was like going to a Hollywood party. The person with the invitation invited someone whose reputation would make them look good and who could introduce them to famous, powerful and useful people.

I had none of these things to offer Jean-Paul.

Even if *The Starlet* was a hit, I couldn't cope with Hollywood

life. The parties made my skin crawl. The people terrified me.
Like Eric Sargeant had said, Hollywood was a game—but I
didn't know how to play it.

I signed the paper and wondered what I was doing with my
life.

JUNE 28. Wedding day. Fifty guests mingled in Grams's garden. It was in full bloom: bougainvillea, honeysuckle, delphiniums, gardenias, roses—Grams's miniature Versailles. Tutu ran between the poppies and sniffed well-polished shoes. Cocktails were served off to one side and the ceremony was to take place under an enormous weeping willow.

I looked out the bedroom window at the guests three floors below—Z, Eric, P. La Roche, Laurence (Maurice Goldschmidt was in Zurich on business), Mom, Chanda. The rest were friends of Jean-Paul's family. There was Sacha! My palms began to sweat. I felt hot. I glanced in the mirror at my red face, then looked back down at Sacha. Why couldn't I be marrying him? At least he had shown up. As Z had said, my sex life needn't end with marriage.

Where was Jean-Paul? I wanted to compare the two. Ah, there he was, dashing in black tails and talking to an effervescent Candice, dressed as if she'd stepped out of a Renoir. Jean-Paul was infinitely more handsome, but my heart didn't palpitate like it did for Sacha. It was the way Sacha moved, the sensuous gestures of his hands. He was wearing that same navy three-piece pinstriped suit, flirting with Chanda, feeling her shoulder pads. She had him cornered between the rose bushes and the herb garden. I laughed. I didn't care. He had come to see me. As long as I could think he loved me more than anyone when we were together, what did I care what he did when we were apart? After all, I was the one marrying someone else.

I downed my third glass of champagne. No day like today for champagne. So what if Jean-Paul had insisted on that prenuptial. That was yesterday. I was going to enjoy my wedding, my triumph. As Jean-Paul had said, what did that paper matter if I wasn't marrying him for his money—and I wasn't. I was marrying him to make Sacha jealous and to have a new life, a safe haven. I wouldn't have to battle the world and struggle to make it—whatever *it* was—anymore. What a way to give up—marrying a millionaire, a handsome, famous millionaire!

I heard Tutu's paws on the staircase. Grams followed. "*Ooh-ooh*," she said in her singsong voice, her way of saying hello. Grams had spent the previous day in the salon dusting, polishing, removing plastic, checking for scratches. Tutu scampered into the bedroom and smelled my feet. Laurence, Grams and Mom followed, chatting and waving their hands around as if they were long-lost friends. They dressed me in my ivory satin gown with its six-foot train which P. La Roche had added for the ceremony. A thin cream-colored veil covered my eyes. My hair was pulled back into a chignon. A satin pillbox was centered on my head.

"That dress is awfully low cut, Maya," my mother said.

Grams, not understanding English, nodded her head in agreement. "*Oui, oui, elle est très jolie.*"

Tutu wagged his tail.

"Mrs. Dunkelburger," Laurence interjected with a smile, "that's the style today."

"Well, in my—" Mom stopped. She was outnumbered.

My mother had wanted to go to the Paris Hilton, or preferably a motel, where she could feel at home. She didn't like foreigners, so she said, though she wouldn't leave Grams's side and appeared to be in awe of Laurence.

The string quartet began Brahms's *Ave Maria*—my favorite if you're going to have an *Ave Maria*. Laurence, Grams and Mom held my train. We four women descended the spiral staircase. Tutu followed, barking, wagging his stub of a tail. He had never been to a wedding before and thought this was a party for him in his own dear bathroom—Grams's garden.

We went through the French doors opening onto the terrace. Jean-Paul was waiting there for me, looking like a proud husband-to-be. With his brown hair, dark blue eyes and black tuxedo with satin trim and red cummerbund, he had the majesty of Velázquez's painting of the royal family. Tears fell from both his eyes. Real tears. Now Jean-Paul could make the family he never really had. He could be the father and husband Alessandro never was able to be.

Everyone became silent. The minister, a friend of Grams's, began the vows. I heard Jean-Paul say, "I do." My turn next. I looked at the guests, spotted Sacha, looked back to Jean-Paul and said, "I do." A tear fell on my cleavage. Jean-Paul thought it was for him. Sacha knew it was for him. Didn't he?

Jean-Paul slipped the ring on my finger. I felt relief; I felt rich. I turned to the guests and threw the bridal bouquet of white roses and baby's breath. Chanda, standing next to Sacha, caught it, embraced him, then kissed him on the lips. Tutu lifted his leg and peed on his suit pants. Sacha frowned and went to the bar for a Perrier to launder his tainted trousers. Jean-Paul guided me through the guests to Grams and my mother. I grabbed a glass of champagne.

"Elsie Mae," Jean-Paul said, "how's it feel to have a married daughter?"

"I don't know yet," Mom laughed, shrugging her shoulders, flashing her one dimple. "How do you say plastic in French?"

"Plastic is *plas-tique*."

"I am trying to tell Madame Gringa—"

"Grinda, Mom," I said.

"Madame Grinda, my living room and that of my own mother's farmhouse—that's in Pottstown, Pennsylvania—are covered in plastic too. Except for family reunions. Once a year."

"Ah, *bon*," Grams said. "*C'est pratique. Une bonne idée.*"

"Oon bunny day," Mom said, nodding her head.

Jean-Paul could see we were not needed and took my hand. Someone grabbed my elbow. Sacha! Candice was by his side. I trembled.

"Maya, allow me to congratulate you and the groom," he said. (Ha! The groom, I thought. No flowery compliment for Jean-Paul. He was jealous!) "May I introduce Candice McIlhenney." (I almost said no!)

A calm, confident Candice extended her hand. Her dark brown hair glistened in the sun. Her skin was whipped-cream white. Her clear blue eyes framed by thick black lashes stared into mine. No trace of envy. No games. Her serenity made her even more beautiful.

I felt nauseated.

Chanda, who had been following Sacha, took his hand. "Come meet the designer of the wedding dress!"

Candice turned to Jean-Paul and said, "Congratulations. May I kiss the groom?" For some reason I wasn't consulted. Nor did I get my kiss from Sacha. I would fix that. Candice's lips rested on Jean-Paul's long enough for me to count the fifty guests. What did she matter? I was his wife, No. 1. Where was Sacha? On the other side of the garden, you could bet, cooing with P. La Roche and Chanda.

I was glad I had my ring and my champagne.

Z grabbed my shoulders from behind, turned me around and kissed both my cheeks. "Well, Baby Snooks grows up."

Jean-Paul excused himself and walked to the bar with Candice. He didn't like Z.

I was happy he had left. I needed Z's help—to be alone with Sacha. When I signed Jean-Paul's prenuptial agreement, I signed away any guilt about continuing my sex life with Sacha. Jean-Paul had his terms; I had mine. Just like Laurence.

"Thanks, Z, for getting Sacha here. You do good work."

"*Très facile.* Still hot to trot?" Z looked in Sacha's direction.

"How? Where?"

"Harold Robbins suggests bathrooms in a pinch."

"When?"

"Try now."

Z grabbed my hand and pulled me toward Sacha. He extricated himself from a clinging, blinking Chanda, who slithered off to the bar. When he looked at me, my jealousy vanished. His eyes told me I was the one he wanted. "Maya, you look ravishing. I only wish I were part of the ceremony. You become more beautiful each day."

Z smiled. "Wait till you see the loo. It's beautiful too. Why don't you show Sacha the inside of your big, beautiful, purple and green throne."

"*Ça va*, Sacha?" I managed to say.

"I can only give you my wedding present in private, madame," he said.

"Off with you then," said Z. "I'll guard the garden with Supertoots."

Sacha followed me to Chanda's bathroom and gave me the biggest, best wedding present of all. Even kissing was painful. I knew I would miss those lips. The loo became a palace. King Sacha unzipped my dress, hung it up, took off his pants and neatly hung them up too. He put the purple toilet seat down. He was ready with his wedding present. Never had he been hung like this before. He held me by my waist, stared at my postnuptial pubic hairs, parted them with his delicate fingers and began his repast.

I held on to his shoulders. His head. I moaned. His fingers penetrated. Everywhere. I was still wearing my pillbox hat, my white gloves, my white garter belt and white stockings. Spreading my legs, he pulled me on top of him and pushed me down, up and down, up and down gently in time with the sounds of the string quartet. Why didn't Sacha have Jean-Paul's money? Why couldn't I paste them together? Why couldn't Jean-Paul give head like Sacha? Visions were spinning. My eyes closed. I held on to the toilet chain hanging from the ceiling. Sacha's face appeared on Jean-Paul's body. I heard a sound, a loud cry . . . a gurgle, a cough. A muffled scream. My own. I pulled the chain. Sacha had shoved his hand over my mouth. I felt muzzled and wild, but we laughed. Sacha loved to laugh.

"Darling, some good news. I'm moving to Paris very shortly to film that project I told you about."

"Wonderful. You got the financing?"

"Yes, Darian arranged it. I had to put her in the lead, of course."

"Oh." I was angry. I had been hoping he would give me the part. But now it didn't matter, since I'd quit acting. Still, he could have asked me. Obviously Sacha and Darian had resumed their affair. Maybe they had never stopped.

A serene Sacha returned to the guests while I stepped into the bedroom and changed into a lavender suit, *grand-mère*'s wedding present to me.

Moments later Jean-Paul and I drove off in his new Porsche. On to Brittany. Our honeymoon.

What had I done? Now, making love to Jean-Paul would take some adjusting. When I closed my eyes I could try to pretend he was Sacha. At least with the aid of my pills and alcohol I could. The eucalyptus trees lined the two-lane highway and seemed to be planted by Godly design—equidistant, all the same height, continuing for miles. The air was clean and sunlight clear. Cool in June. I felt cool. Cool toward Jean-Paul. But I would make it work. In time I would forget Sacha.

We stopped at Mont-Saint-Michel. The clouds rolled in. The fortress looked like a floating peak. Waves crashed against the rocks. I needed sun, and suggested we push onward. The southern coast of Brittany ought to be sunny, calm, and filled with chubby women wearing big white hats and colorful costumes. They would sell waffles and ice cream. We would stay a few days at the Hôtel Griffon and gorge on *langouste grillée au beurre blanc*.

Eat. Eat. Eat. That was our honeymoon. The last night I didn't take a pill or drink much wine. I tried to make it work.

After all, Jean-Paul had one thing over Sacha. One thing only. He did love my breasts. And they loved him. Each night he would talk to them. Like two bellflowers. Together. Apart. When he held the left one in his hand I would say, childlike, "Don't pay too much attention to her. The right one gets jealous." And sure enough it would shrivel up like a dried raisin. I hated my nipples like that. Men thought I was turned on— when I was turned off. Turned on, my nipples looked like pink puffy marshmallows with their tiny blue veins trying to flow out of the flesh. But no matter how much attention my breasts got, or how much money they had made as Miss Bali, Miss Maidenform, etc., I still didn't feel they were good enough for men. I had perfect 34B's. I wanted more perfect 36C's. And big dark brown nipples, like a Negress. Not delicate pink ones like mine. I loved those pictures of tribal women—Ubangi, Watusi —with their proud burnt-almond nips.

I believed Jean-Paul when he told me my breasts were beautiful. That's what Jean-Paul did for me that Sacha didn't. Sacha just wasn't a tit man. Oh, yes, he liked to brush them, shove them, swing them against his better self when I kissed him there. That he liked. But Sacha never talked to my titties.

I began to kiss Jean-Paul, moving down, down, down. His was healthy-looking and smooth, covered with long brown hairs that sometimes got in my teeth. It had a virginal quality, a purity. Few veins, well hidden by thick, tough skin. Shiny skin, like I imagined a Japanese samurai's might be. The happy, contented cock of a young boy, a proud boy.

"Sit on me," Jean-Paul said, as though he'd read my mind.

He held my waist and slowly moved me up and down. I closed my eyes and again thought of Sacha. Sacha's prize. His most valuable possession. Sacha's was thick, one of the biggest

I'd experienced. With bulging purple and blue-black veins, bursting with force. Throbbing with energy. The thrust of his mind. A warrior. Full of his own madness. His obsessions. All of Sacha's charms, passions and secrets were stored here. Locked. Guarded. I had one key, but who cared? Keys were out everywhere. Sacha's was meant to give pleasure and to get it. From many. To many. Made for that. Not to be saved, or burdened with guilt, or married. Just a big well-hung champion, an honest-to-God philandering cock.

He would shout, "Stop, I'm too hot . . . too hot . . . wait!" And sure enough that crimson cock would fade from fire to flesh and slowly settle down for its siesta, matinee, nap, only to reappear when Sacha felt able to be in control.

But the closer we became, the less he cared about control. He had abandoned his fears. That was love, and that was when I felt most loved.

I felt Jean-Paul's throbbing deep inside me. Thank God for my mind, my imagination, my secrets. The cock in my mind. No one could take it away. No one could own it. I didn't have to think right! Or please Sacha or Jean-Paul inside my head. There I was free. I cried. I came.

Jean-Paul kissed me. "I love you."

"And I love you," I half-lied. And sleep fell upon us.

Our honeymoon was over.

FOUR months later, my life had become lunch, lunch, more lunch. Alone. Always alone. Lunching at four-star restaurants had been a fantasy that did not include a dog as my sole companion. I loved Tutu, but our mutual interests were limited. Lunching alone was depressing, but it was something to do.

Le Grand Véfour, Tour d'Argent, Chez Allard, La Coupole, La Closerie des Lilas, Brasserie Lipp, Le Relais Athénée. Never Maxim's. I had grown from a size 8 to a size 11.

"Maya, I don't want to be seen at Maxim's," Jean-Paul would say. "It's too bourgeois, you understand."

I didn't understand. He never objected to any other restaurant. Furthermore, when we first met he had told me flippantly, "I've been brought up in a very classy bourgeois way." Then he'd laughed. "I'm not a Brooklyn ruffian, you know." If Jean-Paul were bourgeois, why would he resent a restaurant that was bourgeois? Afraid of his temper, I didn't argue.

We had moved from Grams's back to our newly furnished apartment by the Invalides. The decor, chosen by Jean-Paul, consisted of objects from his childhood. Eleven rooms covering two hundred square meters occupied by two people and a toy poodle.

Each day Jean-Paul was up early, then met with the lawyers, then played tennis with the lawyers. Each night we dined, often with Tutu, at a different restaurant—usually of my choosing

from the *Gault & Millaut* monthly, which rated the newest bistros. Many nights Jean-Paul was too tired to go out. Nevertheless, after a little coaxing, he would change his mind. With each
meal I tasted a new apéritif, wine or brandy, part of my post-
graduate credits in sophistication.

After a few glasses of wine I was ready to question Jean-Paul
about his day. "I don't want to talk about business," he'd say. Or
he'd reply, "I'm exhausted. You don't like to read good books.
Don't pretend to c-c-care about my father's manuscripts." He
was shutting me out of his life once more, just as he had in the
past.

I was rich. I had credit to buy anything. So why didn't I feel
rich? I became bored so easily with everything and everyone.
Never good at small talk in any language, I had no friends and
didn't know how to make them. *Parisiens* are about as friendly as
the inhabitants of a morgue. In fact, Paris reminded me of a
morgue. A city obsessed with its tombs, its monuments, its
past. Visiting monuments alone was more lonely than lunching
alone. I wanted to enjoy today. But it was always raining. Rain,
rain that never went away. Sunshine was something I went to
the movies to see in films made in southern California. I fantasized about sunlight. That white Los Angeles light. The sound
of warm weather. The stillness of those Santa Ana desert winds.

Laughter was something else I went to the movies for. Laughter and smiles. *Parisiens* pushed and shoved and wore buttons
that said "Smile" while they frowned. I missed agent Michael
Stone's phony toothy grin. "Patronize me, la France! Go ahead
and patronize me! Pretend you're Japanese," would be my
bumper sticker of choice.

Parisiens hated each other. And they especially hated Ameri-
cans. My attitude didn't help me to make friends either.

At Grams's suggestion, I joined an aerobics class on the *cin-
quième étage* of 12, Boulevard Malesherbes. Tutu watched. The
room, complete with a ballet barre and mirrored walls, was
straight out of a Degas. (Who needed museums when inspiration

for art was all around?) That was the good part.

But when I finished my workout and was sweaty, tired and smelled foul, there was no Jacuzzi, steambath, sauna—or even shower! I would long for the outdoor swimming pool and all the facilities of my gym on Santa Monica Boulevard in Hollywood, California.

After a few aerobics classes, Tutu and I quit and decided with that part of the afternoon we would have tea instead. We visited hotel lobbies. Sitting in the Ritz, the Crillon, the Georges V, the Plaza-Athénée, with Tutu on my lap eyeing a chocolate *glace*, or having tea *avec citron* with a Mont Blanc on the side, amused us for a while. We would study the decor, listen to the different languages, take in the latest fashions and try to distinguish the clientele from the hookers. Sometimes I would fantasize about flashing a valet in an elevator, but with Tutu following me around that never happened. He was my bodyguard. Some days I'd cover for him. He didn't like the scent of Arabs and would attack their kaftans. We were thrown out of a four-star hotel more than once.

When Jean-Paul was out of town—he went to Italy often— we stayed home and watched French telly. There was only one movie in English each week. It always seemed to be *King Kong*. Tutu didn't mind. I would open a bottle of wine and stare at the pages of a fashion magazine in disgust, remembering the twenty-eight cable stations I had at my fingertips in L.A.

Though Jean-Paul didn't want me to continue acting, he wanted me to continue studying. "You must find something constructive to do with your time," he would nag. I joined an English-speaking workshop in scene study near the Panthéon filled with students from the Sorbonne, and once more at the ripe old age of thirty-three felt out of it—even though I'd heard from Zercon Films that the previews of *The Starlet* had high ratings. After a few sessions at the Ecole du Théâtre with expe-rienced younger actors who insisted on speaking French, I quit. Sitting in hotel lobbies was more fun and a real course in scene study. Why fool myself? I would never be able to act in Paris because I would never be able to speak French without an accent.

Oh, I studied French each day, but I knew I would never speak it well enough to be spared the ridicule of *Parisiens*. Socially, I had learned it was better to speak English than grope French. I valued my conversations with Tutu and those moments with a cab driver when I was forced to speak his language, yet didn't feel belittled. I loved the working class but despised the bourgeoisie.

Grand-mère and Laurence were two exceptions. But Grams and I had too many generations between us, and Laurence was always jetting off somewhere. So was Jean-Paul. When he wasn't with the lawyers on Avenue Wagram, he was visiting one of Alessandro's castles in Italy. Each of the nine had to be inventoried. Italy was going to build a museum in honor of Alessandro, paid for by the Nobel Prize winner's estate—a tax hedge.

With Jean-Paul gone five days of the week, I was more lonely than ever. Each morning to get out of bed I needed the maid to bring me a Bloody Mary. She swore she wouldn't tell Jean-Paul.

The only thing that really held my interest was sex. But not with Jean-Paul. If I drank enough at dinner, I would pass out in his arms and avoid the issue altogether. Jean-Paul and I never talked about our feelings, our angers. We just kept living with our masks on, like any other unhappily married couple.

Thank God I had Sacha's letters. He would write me care of the greengrocer's. The owner, a former member of the Resistance, loved the intrigue. Sacha wrote twice a week. I hid his letters in my old modeling portfolio, now dusty, behind the photos.

He would be arriving in October to begin his film. I kept a calendar by my bed and marked off each day. Jean-Paul thought I was checking my period, practicing the rhythm method. He didn't want children yet, he said.

I didn't know what I wanted—except Sacha's arms.

• • •

Then at last it was October 10, the day Sacha would be arriving. He had rented a suite in a small hotel facing Notre Dame, on the Ile Saint-Louis. We were to rendezvous in the room, on the bed. I was to arrive first.

I was dressed like one of Toulouse-Lautrec's tawdry yet adorable whores. Once I had visited the Jeu de Paume solely to study his models' makeup and lingerie.

A green velvet love seat and wormwood armoire were the only pieces of furniture in the bedroom. The brass bed faced a full-length antique mirror. A braided carpet covered the floor. Sunlight streamed through the French windows. Blackbirds flew by. I looked at a barge moving along the Seine as a storm gathered in the distance. Paris always seemed to have a storm gathering in the distance.

Birds chirped. A burst of sunlight on the white comforter reflected warmth on my face. I felt safe with the thought of Sacha coming home. Home to me. I missed him, missed his funny round body, his hairy back and chest, his silly big Dumbo-like ears, his blue eyes and raspy voice, his lips with the most perfect touch, his smell. When he was deep in thought, he perspired. Concentration oozed out of his pores. I wanted to eat his mind. Consume him. Oh, where was he?

I heard the *ascenseur*. Footsteps. Posing like the Naked Maja, I lay back on the bed and inhaled.

Wearing his navy three-piece suit, a longer-haired Sacha entered, closed the door behind him and stood at the foot of the bed between the brass pillars.

"Well, well, well, my dear, who have we here? Madame Récamier? I see France suits you. My, my. Turn over, my pet, and let me see the rest of you."

I liked taking orders from Sacha. Pleasing Daddy Sacha. How could I have made him pay the $20,000? I thought of Candice. Shame vanished.

I rolled over onto all fours, posed with my thirty-eight-inch hips and shook their twelve extra pounds.

"You look marvelous, my dear. Complete. With the fullness of a fine dessert." Sacha's hands felt my cheeks. "I've missed you," he said to my buttocks. I didn't mind.

"Don't ever go away from me, Sacha. I can't bear to be here without you."

"My darling, I'm here now. That's all that matters."

When I was with Sacha, I felt safe. But at home, if that was the right word, I felt in the way. Jean-Paul's temper was escalating. When I bought something he didn't like, he would explode with rage, so I rarely took anything out of a shop without his approval.

Shopping had become boring. When you can buy anything you want, you want very little because everything looks the same. Nevertheless, I shopped on.

One day I bought a pair of alligator pumps Jean-Paul had approved. When the salesgirl asked, "Where would you like these delivered, madame?" with delight I mentioned Jean-Paul's name. "*Vraiment?*" she laughed, and glanced at the other *vendeuses*, who were checking me out from head to toe, snickering. Trembling, I had trouble signing the check. Why had I thought I would get satisfaction from someone else's fame?

It was beginning to rain. I ran to a café on the Boulevard Raspail. I was crying. Why did I care what a salesgirl said? Who was I? Why didn't I have something of my own? I knew *The Starlet* would be a bomb. I drank my wine, finished it and ordered another. Women were supposed to be happy married to millionaires. I looked at the couples sharing umbrellas. They were smiling. I wondered where Jean-Paul was. Maybe I did love him and didn't know it. Then I remembered he was at the estate counting his lire. And Sacha? Where was Sacha? On the Champs-Elysées counting his film crew. And what was I counting? My drinks.

I sat in the glass-enclosed café watching traffic. Taxis were honking. A *deux-chevaux* sped by and splashed a handsome couple sharing a large navy blue umbrella like the one I had bought Jean-Paul. The couple was laughing. His arm was around her waist. He was protecting her from the cars, the rain, the people. He cared. She was beautiful. She looked familiar. The glass streaked with rain blurred the images. They were only a few feet away. I put on my glasses. It was Jean-Paul and Candice!

I put my hands over my head and pretended to be reading. There was nothing to read. It didn't matter. They hadn't noticed me. They were laughing, hugging, and as they walked off he kissed her playfully just like he kissed me. Why did I care? I did. I ordered another glass of wine. So that was why Jean-Paul stayed so late at the estate. That's why he was there on weekends. That's why he rarely lunched with me. How could I complain? I would call Sacha tonight. Now I was feeling dizzy. Sick. I began walking. Nowhere. Anywhere. Stumbling along the cobblestones. Umbrellas jabbed at me. Without one I was defenseless. I shoved on my sunglasses to protect my eyes. My silk shirt was soaked, now transparent.

At a crosswalk I slipped and fell into the gutter. I didn't want to get up. Lightning crackled. Cars splashed. I tasted mud. I felt dizzy, like I was swimming in a river between the sidewalk and the road.

Three Algerians extended their hands. I didn't want help. When you don't want men, I thought, they're there, but when you want one, just one, lots of luck! I stood up, rubbed my hands covered in cinders on my once tan suede skirt and continued through the crowd. A blur of angry umbrellas. Congested Montparnasse.

I turned down an alley. The smell of couscous. More Algerians ran between raindrops. The sky blackened. Thunder. A *tabac!* I needed cigarettes.

It was a tiny shop filled with magazines, soda pop, international pacifiers for oral or sexual frustration. France's answer to

Seven-11. By the register stood a toothless Arab with a curly black moustache. He smiled, proud of his gums. The left side of his face was crimson, badly burned. His shirt, unbuttoned to his navel, revealed a hairy chest flaunting gold chains. As he pushed out his stomach, a roll of fat fell over his trousers. Gold rings covered his tobacco-stained fingers.

He said something and waved his hands excitedly. I didn't understand. He was a happy fool. I envied him. This dirty, cluttered shop was his palace. He leered. Maybe he envied me. I picked up a pack of Gauloises and began leafing through maga-zines. I had no place to go. No shop to run. No husband who wanted me. No lover who needed me. Let it rain. Let him watch. I felt him studying me while I studied *Vogue, Elle*. Bor-ing. Young beauties thrown into garments they'd never wear, tolerating hours of verbal and physical abuse, suffering with a smile. A paid-for, expensive smile. What had been my price? I couldn't remember. I couldn't remember a lot. Now I was mod-eling for Mr. Algiers. For free. For fun and for free. *Clop, clop, clop*. He played with his worry beads.

I dropped *Elle* and scanned the newsstand. Stacks of girlie magazines covered the center shelf. I loved smut. In Hollywood I had hidden *High Society* and *Penthouse* under my bed, and I had lived alone. Looking at the forbidden turned me on. I loved anything dirty. What was dirty? What Mom didn't approve of. Dirty books. Dirty men. That's why I loved Sacha. We did the forbidden. I picked up an issue with a cover of a naked woman in chains. The *clop, clop* stopped. Now rustling. Mr. Algiers, still guarding his register, was holding up a magazine. His favor-ite monthly.

"*Américaine?*" he asked, staring at my breasts. I looked down and saw my nipples protruding through wet saffron-colored silk. That tingling began, that ringing. I felt drawn to the black-foot. I stood across the counter and looked down at the magazine.

"*Pornographie, pornographie,*" he said, smiling and pointing to a photo of two men having sex with a woman seated in some leather device I had never seen before. He pointed to her face. *Clop, clop* went the worry beads. I didn't need his pointing. I noticed her expression right away. Ecstasy. She was having a good time. A very good time. Suddenly I felt as if I were in an oven. Baking. Rising. Something was rising. I wanted to be naked. Like her. Free. Bad. I leaned on the counter and pushed my breasts together with my elbows, like I had done modeling for all those liquor ads. He gazed into my cleavage. My famous cleavage. He smelled of garlic. Too much ratatouille. What next? Flashing took planning, calculating. That was part of the fun. Writing the scene in my mind. Then came the direction. I felt my breasts and unbuttoned a few buttons.

"Non!" he said. He signaled me to follow him. Mr. Algiers was afraid he might look bad to his customers, his neighbors, the police. Or lose a sale of Dubble Bubble. So we crept to the back of the shop through crates, boxes, papers, debris. His fear lost my respect. I would have done it right there. He was the coward. Most of them were. That was part of the game. What turned me on most. Testing their shame. Their threshold. Their fear of public opinion. What if they were caught watching me? Wasn't that bad? Why wasn't that a crime as well? I couldn't flash alone. That was masturbation and A-OK, but when someone watched me enjoying myself, their watching made me bad. I could go to jail for what they did. I laughed. What made sense?

He opened the door to a minuscule bathroom. Airwick overpowered me. He closed the door and locked it. I put the toilet seat down. Neon illuminated cobwebs and a blood-stained wall. I needed a drink. This would be my drink. Once I touched myself, Dr. Winston's famous clit job, it wouldn't matter where I was. I'd forget it all. I pulled off my skirt and panties, laid them on the seat and sat on top. "Never sit on a toilet seat without covering it," Mom would say.

Mr. Algiers still held the magazine. Fuck that, I thought, grabbing it from him. He pulled it back, pointing to a photo of a black man shoving his cock into a white woman's mouth. "No!" I shouted, pointing to the floor. I wanted him on his knees.

What had I gotten myself into? I didn't like the locked door. But I could handle him. Always did. Like I did the delivery man.

I leaned back and spread my legs. He dropped the magazine and knelt on the dirt floor like a good boy. A roach crawled by. I screamed. He laughed. I liked him. He was sweet.

"Prittee," he said. "You very prittee."

"I know, you asshole," I said with a smile.

He smiled back. Ignorance could be this. He was squeezing my thighs. That wasn't allowed. He was spreading them. That was allowed.

I began to rub. He unzipped his fly and began to rub. He had warts all over his giant Algerian prick. This was another adventure. More information. History. It beat going to the library. Anyway his warty cock would never be in me. That was only for Sacha and Jean-Paul. That kind of sex was different, required a different sort of man. Flashing was reserved for the servants of the world. I was giving pleasure to the deprived— the Marie Antoinette of perversions, a perverse Florence Nightingale, freeing the less fortunate from their sexual guilt. I liked turning on the poor and deformed. And I was good at it. Feeling superior to them was part of the thrill. I rarely felt superior. But jerking off in front of someone like Mr. Algiers made me feel momentarily worthy.

His eyes took in my pink dewy lips. I squeezed, released. Squeezed, released. Showed him what he'd be in store for if he got a better job, as my mother used to say, an education. Millionaires, Hollywood directors, producers, these men had the pleasure of my tight lips. Mr. Algiers could only watch. But who knows, someday he could be the next Louis B. Mayer. You never knew about Hollywood.

A black spider crept up my arm. "Oh," I cried. He brushed it off and killed it. Now he was Lenny from *Of Mice and Men*. Oh, he was a sweetheart. I was so afraid of spiders. They reminded me of eight penises with one mind. That I couldn't control.

His black hair brushed against my thighs. He wanted to taste me. "No, no," I said as though he were a naughty pet.

He honored my wishes and rubbed on. I thought how wicked this was. What if Jean-Paul knew? What if Mom knew? They'd freak! Some part of me wanted them to know the real me. Sacha would have liked to watch. Sacha liked me to tell him about all the men I had been with. Especially these men. This made me feel close to Sacha. He didn't judge me or make me feel ashamed. Instead he liked my insanity.

I knew this was nuts. Who was I fooling? Watching Jean-Paul with another woman put a kink in my day. In me. In my cunt. I wasn't good in bed anymore. And I needed to be the best. With everyone, whether I loved them or not. Well, Jean-Paul needed someone new. A new thrill. Then so did I. Today was my Battle of Algiers. War made me feel connected. Whole. Because I always won.

Screams. Mine. It was over, and I was out. Lickety-split.

Walking down the street, I lit up a Gauloise. Damn! I'd forgotten to pay for them.

I hailed a cab, went back to our apartment, polished off the vodka and crawled into bed. Tutu followed, and we both passed out.

"What's with Sleeping Beauty?" Jean-Paul shouted as he turned on the lights.

My head ached. "What time is it?"

"Eight. We're having dinner with the Italian ambassador. You haven't forgotten?"

"I don't feel up to it."

"*Mais, chérie,* you must."

"No, I mustn't."

Jean-Paul stood over the bed, hands on hips, a look of fury on his suddenly red face. "You're drunk!"

"No, I'm not," I said, pouting. "Well, a little." I feigned a giggle.

"How did you g-get like this?" he shouted. His eyes wanted to spring from their sockets. He rolled his upper lip into his gums, biting on his lower lip.

"Sitting in a café on Boulevard Raspail watching my husband and another woman walk by," I sang sarcastically to Simon and Garfunkel's "Homeward Bound."

He walked to the window.

"How's Candice, J.P.? No time for me at lunch? Business, business, but time for phony socialites like Candice McIlhenney? Thought you didn't like to be seen with Hollywood trash?"

"Look, Maya, I can do as I please. You have a good life. What are you complaining about? So what if I saw Candice today? She's a friend."

"Sure. A friendly cunt."

Jean-Paul slapped me. Tutu growled. Jean-Paul kicked him across the room. Tutu whimpered. "Listen, you've been sitting around this apartment for four months. Not making friends. Not working. Not trying. Most women would kill to be in your shoes. You're starring in a movie coming out. What do you want?"

"Companionship and someone who doesn't slap me around when I don't do what he wants."

"You'll never be s-satisfied."

"Why don't you put your checkbook around me and add a leash?"

Jean-Paul lunged toward the bed.

"You ingrate!" He pulled me up and shook me. "Stay in bed all night! I don't want you at the dinner." He threw me back down on the bed. My head hit the wall. I heard Tutu whimper and passed out.

When I awoke the next day, Jean-Paul was already at the lawyers'. Tutu was limping. I took him to the vet. Bad news. He might need an operation. I left him there and called Sacha at his hotel. "Darling, Tutu will be all right. Why don't you come over? I'm working on my script, but I would love to see you."

Sacha would make me feel better. I needed him, his love and support. But he could only see me once a week, he said, because of his filming schedule. I would visit the various locations around Paris—Trocadéro, Invalides, Boul' Mich, Au Printemps, Les Halles—but I would feel in the way, because I *was* in the way. When he flirted with the script girl, the makeup artist, the hairdresser, the actresses—especially Darian Nelson, who was cool to me—my skin would turn green. Furthermore, I had to arrange these visits when Candice would not be there. No. 2. Always number two. That was me.

For one hour of our weekly matinee we would fight about the mythical affairs I accused him of having—mythical, my size 7 triple A foot!

Today I would not pick a fight, I thought as I took the elevator to the fourth floor. I pushed the iron gates back and stepped onto the landing. I tapped on the door. Sacha embraced me.

"What have I married, Sacha?" I cried.

"My darling, you've married a bank. He's worth it. Adjust. We all have to feel worthy of having money. You've never been in this position before."

"Oh, it's not the money, Sacha. It's his temper. He kicked Tutu last night." I was afraid to tell him Jean-Paul beat me, afraid because Sacha might not care.

"He'll be OK. What you need is some love, which I'm going to give you with great pleasure."

I loved it when Sacha told me what to do, think, feel. I liked being under his thumb. Feeling like his servant. But I hated that game out of bed.

Sacha undressed me, then himself. He began his usual sexual operation, and when it was over I felt wonderful. Moments later he slipped out of bed and said, "Well, I'm going to have to get back to the script, Maya. Our shooting schedule is way behind. You understand."

I didn't.

He picked up my coat, kissed me on the cheeks, tapped me on the bum and opened the door. And closed the door.

How could I allow him to treat me this way? How could I allow Jean-Paul to treat me the way he was treating me? One was for money. The other for sex. They both made me sick. I wanted to get away from both of them.

I took a cab to the Café Flore and sat in the back, where the view was the best. I wanted to watch. Watching helped me to forget. So did martinis.

I pulled out an unopened letter from Zercon Films. Rave reviews for *The Starlet*. Big deal. I wanted rave reviews from Sacha. Without reading the details, I crumpled the notices and dropped them on the floor.

Why was I letting a sixty-four-year-old man make me feel old, useless, had? I downed the martini. My anger didn't disappear as it usually did. My joints felt heavy. I puffed on a Gauloise. My head ached. The tuxedoed waiters went in and out of focus. I squinted. The room became a pointillist painting. If only I were home in bed. But I didn't want to risk running into Jean-Paul.

Four o'clock in the afternoon. Students were arriving from the Sorbonne. They laughed, slapped each other on the back. They studied, cared, had purpose. Hope. They were young.

I remembered an affair I had had in Hollywood with a director. Like most men in positions of power, he was married more to his work than to his wife. In the morning he would jump out of bed and pull out a schedule that his secretary had typed for his day. Boastfully he would show it to me. Then he was out the door. Finished with me. I had served my purpose. My cunt had been my purpose, though it was not typed on the schedule. I envied this piece of paper, his having a secretary, his having a purpose. What was my purpose? Sex. I was one more item in his day. An item.

I looked at the ashtray.

This was how Sacha treated me as well. These men didn't care about my feelings. Why was I addicted to them? To get them to leave their women and rescue me? To get them to love me? Why couldn't I just fuck them like they fucked me?

I wanted to be more than my cunt. I *was* more than my cunt. But most men didn't think so. That was the problem. Or so I told myself.

Jean-Paul had the estate and his lawyers. Sacha had his film crew and Candice. I had Tutu, and pills and alcohol. I didn't give a rat's ass about *The Starlet*. The room spun. Perspiration oozed from the back of my neck. My armpits stank. I inhaled the final drag, vowed that would be my last cigarette and ordered another martini.

Acting was more victimizing. Cunt-flaunting. There was no way for someone like me—who looked like me, who behaved like me—to be treated with respect or even with a good review. What actress with any sex appeal hadn't had to deal with the casting couch? With the Harry Blydons I had tried to run my own version. But it was empty. Boring. I had begun having sex with Sacha to get a part in his film, and got caught in my own game. Men always won at Casting Couch, whether women spread their legs or not. If the charms of the penis didn't destroy, the rejecting male ego did. One good review in *The Starlet* wouldn't change this.

Most Hollywood moguls thought they had the power of kings. Victimizing starlets and denigrating actresses was an approved spectator sport, while the king's lackeys who procured these women were rewarded by career advancement—particularly when the king met with an exciting, wild, sexually innovative crop of young starlets. As an added perk these lackeys, homely penis-envying males, enjoyed tasting the king's leftovers.

In the king's eyes a starlet having sex with him was performing her royal service. His court—producers, casting directors,

directors—trained, powdered and perfumed the starlets—some talented, some not so talented, but all eager—then paraded them before the king, who chose whom he would audition (fuck), cast (fuck), reject (fuck).

That was another reason I liked flashing. It was getting back at all those counterfeit kings, fat and ugly false deities who exploited women. Flashing was my being a man with men. A queen with her court. When I exposed myself, gave myself pleasure and denied intimacy, I was treating my male victims like those power-hungry kings treated their female victims, like Jean-Paul treated me now that he finally had his hands on his father's loot.

Why did my targets have to be poor, working-class and stupid? Because that's how I felt when I went before, or was brought before, those cunt-thirsty corporate fucks—poor and stupid.

A fat man seated to my left blew cigar smoke in my face. I waved the smoke away and signaled for the waiter. Another martini.

I didn't want any part of that life anymore. And that life, the casting couch, was always there for a beautiful actress. When an actress became a star, she would pretend she had never played it, never knew about it, never dirtied those sheets. A successful actress had to lie to protect herself from the sadistic men who ran the motion picture industry. How many women producers, directors, studio heads, chairwomen of the board were there? In Hollywood men networked; homosexual men networked. Did women network? Did they have the power to do so? Female stars who did not speak up only allowed Hollywood's penis power to continue to abuse women.

I looked down at the olive with a toothpick jabbed in its side, smelled the sweet perfumed gin and thought, Or is this all my problem?

I thought of Z. Why, she had been trying to tell me this all along. Make friends with the women, she would say. All those lessons about Hollywood men. She had experienced the same thing. No! This wasn't all my problem. It was every woman's problem. And it wasn't exclusive to Hollywood.

Five o'clock. Students began shouting and singing. Voices felt like electric shocks passing through my brain.

I put the cigarette out, smelled burning flesh and stuck my thumb in my mouth. That was as good a place for it as any, I figured, as I watched the fat man suck his cigar.

I looked at the pimiento wedged into the center of the olive and bit into it. I hated pimientos.

I chipped away at my nail polish and picked my bleeding cuticles. For a television commercial a hand cream company had paid thousands of dollars for my once beautiful hands. Tobacco-stained fingers with torn, chewed nails, flesh bitten to the quick, held the butt of a Gauloise.

Six o'clock. The waiter was ignoring me. Was it my red face? Slurred speech? I signaled for the check. The café was now crowded. It was cocktail hour. A girl with a bald head and a micromini squeezed alongside me on the banquette. I was hot, wet, dizzy. The café felt like the inside of a tomb. No air. Fuck the waiter! Vision blurred. A bald black man. Two. Coming toward me. Fuck the check! I pushed the table aside, stumbled through noisy bodies and reached the sidewalk. Air. That always made it better. Nauseated. I felt nauseated. Why weren't things working that used to? A cab! I jumped inside.

Why did the driver look at me like that? Dizziness. More dizziness. The taxi bounced along the broken road. I held myself between my legs like I did when I was a little girl until I could reach the potty. Too late. Something wet, warm and wet, trickled onto my hand, my skirt, my stockings, my shoes, the vinyl seat. Did the driver know? Could he smell it? I rolled down both windows. We were home. When I stepped out, I gave him a big tip. He felt my wet hand, looked back and said, *"Mon dieu!"*

I quickly buzzed the door to the lobby and ran inside. That nausea again. Oh, where was the elevator? Something growled. My stomach. Something wanted to leave me. I felt cramps. Shooting pains. Doubling over, I stepped into the courtyard a few feet away.

Thank God for darkness. In a corner of the garden I pulled down my pants and squatted. Rot, decay, digested anger, disgust poured out of me. I smelled bile. The past. Beads of perspiration covered my body. I was hot, cold, shaking, trembling. Something mounted. More pain. I leaned over a rosebush and coughed onto the petals. I coughed again. And again. Gagging. Retching. Aching. My insides twisting, squeezing, contracting.

The dizziness stopped. The hot flashes vanished. Peace. Like an animal I had to get away. Away from this part of me. I stood up, pulled up my pants, buttoned my shirt, wiped my mouth.

I couldn't even feel the shame. I was so glad it was over.

I knew I shouldn't have eaten that olive.

The next morning. What a hangover. Pounding. Pressure. My head felt pulverized. I crept to the bathroom and fixed an Alka-Seltzer. That would do it. Then two aspirins and a glass of champagne.

15

AH, a letter came from Z! Hurrah! She would be arriving in one week. Now I would show her what I had been too depressed to show myself—the Luxembourg Gardens, the Orangerie, the Tuileries, the Crazy Horse Saloon—and Maxim's. Too bad what Jean-Paul thought! He didn't have to know everything. Tutu could join us and have the *plat du jour*. I hired a chauffeur for the day. Supertoots and I picked Z up at Orly.

She looked so Hollywood. She had dyed her hair a golden blond and was suntanned and smiling, as usual. My Z. Crazy Z. God, how I missed her.

"La blond bombshell! Glad to see you've only changed your hair color." I laughed as we held each other.

Z pulled away. "Can't you feel my new titties? Thirty-four C's." I studied her breasts. She studied my face. "Well, you ain't exactly fallin' off your *bateau mouche* either, but what's with the white skin and extra L.B.'s?" Z didn't like what she saw.

I changed the subject, my specialty. "I've booked a table at Maxim's. We must check out its new ceiling."

"But of course." Z's frown vanished as she looked into the street, rolling her eyes and wetting her lips. "My, what a lovely Bentley you have, my dear," she said like the Big Good Wolf. "Glad you went for the bucks instead of the bullshit, Maya!"

When we entered the restaurant, to my alarm Tutu was

checked along with my cape and taken to the powder room. Maxim's was *pas de chien*. I had forgotten to check the Guide Michelin. Quickly the maître d' escorted us through a small room filled with women dressed in silk shirts, conservative suits and jewels into an enormous, half-empty ballroom with tapestries on the walls, heavily brocaded chairs and paintings with gold frames. The newly painted ceiling with cupids and drama of its own was barely noticeable. This room was Siberia, but I didn't want Z to know that. Then, too embarrassed to ask what each entrée meant, I ordered two almost identical fish dishes— the cheapest things on the menu. Maybe Sacha was right. I didn't feel worthy of money.

After finishing a bottle of champagne, I stopped pretending. "It's not working, Z. Cinderella didn't get the glass slipper."

"Hey, cutie pie, you've only been married four months."

"I'm lonely, Z. Jean-Paul thinks everyone wants his money and his fame, so we don't have any friends."

"He's probably right. So you make friends. Look, Maya, you're never going to get it all in one man. Take a bit from this one and a bit from that. And you gotta teach men."

"How does Eric feel about that?"

"He does the same. We understand each other. That's why our marriage works."

"What about Chad?"

"Look, I accept I'm the world's worst mom, and so I've hired a great nanny."

"God, I can't accept what time of day it is."

"Well, sweetie, that's your problem, not Jean-Paul."

"He beats me, Z."

"That's not acceptable. What do you do to provoke him?"

"Drink and wander around Paris spying on him and Candice."

"Candice and Jean-Paul?"

"Yep."

"Does Sacha know?"

"No."

"How's it going with the Cossack?"

"A mess there too."

"You need a new lover."

"Lovers and I aren't where it's at. It's so restrictive with Sacha. Same stories, same dialogue. We can't go out because Jean-Paul or Candice might see us—so he says. I don't give a damn if Jean-Paul finds out. I'm tired of Sacha's games."

"Can't you enjoy Sacha just for sex?"

"I want more. I want to feel he cares. He says he loves me, but he doesn't care about my feelings. I want someone who's there emotionally for me, Z. Sacha's emotions are in his cock, and Jean-Paul's are in his bank. The other day I walked along the Seine for three hours without an umbrella and didn't feel the rain."

"I think you need a shrink."

"How could I find a shrink when I can't even find a friend?"

"Someone in L.A. will know. I'll make some calls. By the way, advance word on *The Starlet* is tremendous."

"Z, even if it was a huge hit, I could never act in Paris because of my lousy French. Can you believe I'm beginning to miss L.A.?"

"Easily, Ms. Millionaire, easily. Nice dresses don't turn black skies blue and frowns into smiles. But try to stick it out because of the bucks. The bullshit will always be waiting for you in L.A."

"Did I tell you Sacha wants me to get Jean-Paul to back his next film?"

"Don't ever let a man use you for business. Sex is one thing. But allowing a man to get money out of you is criminal. That's women's work. Never ever let a man use you like we use them. What would happen if men pooled their knowledge?" Z was shouting. "We'd be reduced to slaves."

"Z, I do think you overestimate the importance of money."

"Forget it, Maya! Go smash your Bentley!"

• • •

I was awakened by the sound of the telephone.

"Angel cakes, rise and shine!"

"Oh, Z, thank God."

"You sound horrible."

"I am."

"Here's the number of a shrink. Hollywood's finest. Evelyn Delp. Moved to Paris to get away from the sun. MAI 7149. Got it?"

I fumbled for a pen and paper. The back of an old *Gault & Millaut* would do.

"She's expecting your call in the A.M. Get some sleep. I can amuse myself."

"Sorry, Z."

"Listen, if you need to run away, stay with me. I'll be at the Plaza-Athénée until I run out of francs or St. Laurent runs out of threads."

I fell back to sleep. Tutu lay on my head.

221 Place de la Madeleine. Above Fauchon's. *Le deuxième étage.* A petite dark-haired woman in her late forties greeted me. She was warm and strong. I felt fragile and silly. The office was dimly lit. Two shaded lamps. Photographs of children everywhere.

We talked about men. My need for having one. My need for someone to love me. Evelyn wanted me to learn the difference between love and sex.

Sex with Sacha for sex's sake was OK, she said, if only I would see it for what it was, not what I wanted it to be. I didn't want to get that news.

"But, Evelyn, the other day he asked if I had a pair of jeans for him to cut the crotch out of and have sex in."

"How did you feel about that?"

"Bad. Like a dummy. A whore for the afternoon. Like all he wanted was a body to do things to."

"Did you tell him this?"

"No, I told him I didn't own jeans."

"That's not how one creates intimacy. Yet you say he's not being intimate with you?"

"That's right." I laughed. So this was how blame felt.

"I want you to get some books in assertiveness training. Here's one to start."

She handed me a brown paperback with Mona Lisa smiling at me underneath the title *The Assertive Woman*. I feigned gratitude.

For two weeks I saw Evelyn. The library became my new haunt. Evelyn became my new leader, my guide, my respected companion. *Grand-mère* and I had tea on occasion, and Laurence would invite me to lunch every so often, but I couldn't talk with them about Jean-Paul the way I could to my friend Evelyn. But when I paid her I realized she was no friend. She was a therapist. Well, she was a paid friend, and I figured that had to be worth it. Education and wisdom. Except when she pushed me too far. Then I'd get drunk.

I discovered that going to the library with chilled vodka in a thermos could be fun. I would sit by the stacks with Evelyn's recommended readings and drink myself quietly, pleasantly, pseudo-intellectually into a stupor. The library was transformed into a café. The people were sensual, furtive, good-looking. Minds at work, bodies at rest. While I sipped from my thermos, I fantasized about what I'd like to do sexually to each man and temporarily forgot about my troubles.

Visiting the library filled my days for a while. Sex with Sacha remained the same, but sex with Jean-Paul had fallen apart. Thank God for Quaaludes. Quaaludes would have turned me on to King Kong in drag. I never told Evelyn about my pills. I never told anyone. Except Z. She understood.

Evelyn, by now, had decided that I had stuffed my feelings for Jean-Paul to a point where the relationship was irretrievable. I pretended not to understand. I didn't want to leave him. I wanted his money. Sacha understood. Sacha wanted his money too. That was one thing we both had—if I stayed married.

All the same I would ask myself, What does having money feel like? One afternoon when Jean-Paul was in Italy I went to the bank and withdrew $500,000 in franc notes. That night I went to bed with a bottle of Dom Perignon and covered my naked body from forehead to toenails with francs. Could I now feel money? Surely this was mind-blowing. I fell asleep with the TV on as I did every other night. When I awoke the next day, Tutu had made peepee all over Louis the Fourteenth and his relatives.

I wondered if fame was this difficult to feel. I refused to cover my naked body with eight-by-ten glossies of stars. Tutu had made his point.

The phone had been ringing all morning. Messages from Z and Zercon's publicity department. After grabbing a *café au lait* and a croissant, I called Z.

"Hey, hot tush, how's it feel to be a star?"

"What?"

"Been callin' all A.M. Got golf balls in yer ears? Eric called from sunny southern Cal to say *The Starlet* is boffo . . . top-grossing film first week."

"No," I laughed, cuddling Tutu.

"Yep, lines in Westwood and Hollywood. Sold out every performance. How's it feel to be famous?"

"Don't know. I'm still trying to find out how it feels to be rich."

"Get yourself in shape, fat face, you're gonna have a lot of PR to do."

"No wonder Zercon's been calling."

"Call 'em back. Why'd you call me first, dryer head? Call the Big Beans, PRONTO!"

Click!

Zercon's publicity department was escalating its campaign. Old photos of me were needed for posters.

Would I be photographed and do interviews for magazines and TV? asked Fred, the PR man.

"Yes," I said, assuming if Jean-Paul complained I could always change my mind.

"Your performance is what is selling tickets, Maya, and we at Zercon would like to offer you a private screening for you and your friends."

I preferred seeing it the following week along with an audience when it opened in Paris.

Tutu and I had things to do. Our hair, nails and bodies had to be done. We had to go on a crash diet. No more fancy-pants lunches. One meal a day would keep the kilos away.

The publicity department was going to prep me for interviews.

That night Jean-Paul and I stayed home and watched the telly—his favorite thing to do (yawn!), and later between the sheets I sprung the news. Baby talk worked wonders.

"Maya, this is fantastic," he said, his eyes shining as they had when we first met. "You now have something of your very own. When can we see it?"

"It opens next week. I want to wait to see it with an audience."

He held me, caressing my body as if it were soon to be exhibited in the Louvre. "I'll be in Italy, but I'll catch it in Rome the night it opens and call you."

"You aren't angry? It's rather explicit."

"Why should I be angry? I married you because you're explicit!"

"I've got that on tape, bub, everything you said," I teased—dialogue from a silly TV show I had been in.

When we made love, it was wonderful. I didn't think of Sacha—not too much. So this was how fame felt. I liked it. Maybe now salesgirls would treat me with respect. And maybe Sacha would see more of me and leave Candice.

• • •

The following morning I called Sacha on the set. He was like an expectant father. "My darling, I'd heard the reviews were sensational, but not that you were being singled out. But then, you never have any competition to worry about, precious. You've always been my star."

Sacha and his lines. I wanted his body.

"Well," he continued, "I can see finding you available is going to be difficult."

"Hey, hey, hey, you know all you have to do is..."

We had still been using the kindly services of the greengrocer to get messages to each other when Jean-Paul was in town. The grocer would deliver messages from Sacha along with the other vegetables, inside a head of lettuce.

But I was too busy to see Sacha before the film premiered, and that felt good. There was to be no opening-night celebration, but instead a massive PR campaign. My photo would be on five magazine covers, on posters on buses, in the Métro, on every kiosk. When I walked down the street, people noticed me. I liked the attention. It was forcing me to clean up my act. In five days I lost five pounds.

On opening day of *The Starlet*, I went to meet Z at Ciné-Pathé's Champs-Elysées wearing dark glasses, a blond wig and my maid's uniform. There was a long line to get in, and it was only the three o'clock show. On either side of the theater was a gigantic topless photo of me chained to a bed. The caption— MAYA ENDICOTT IS THE STARLET—covered my naked lap. Why, Zercon hadn't used Jean-Paul's name! How kind.

"Dearie, you will be famous," said Z. By God, she was jealous!

"Will be?" I laughed. "I am!"

I was stunned by the sensationalism of the photos and their size. I could see my nipples without my prescription glasses, even though I couldn't see them when I was naked and looking at myself in the mirror! I loved the defiant spirit in my face and body. The photo had the courage I had lost.

Besides, Z had taught me anything's fair in love and publicity.

PR had no morals, yet it was spiritual. With the right PR an idea could become a reality.

I insisted on sitting in the last row. The credits were done tastefully. Those three days of early rushes that had been poorly lit were cut. The lighting was good. I liked the way I looked. I was superthin. Oh, God, the men were chaining me to the bed, ripping off my clothes. Ten minutes into the film and I was completely naked. It was as though I were watching someone else. Someone I had known. Someone who had guts. I liked the film.

I sneaked out of the theater ten minutes before the end. Z wanted to stay to report the audience's reaction.

Grams! I would call Grams, who had caught the morning show along with Laurence.

I ran to a nearby restaurant, La Lune de Tunis, that had a pay phone and bought a *jeton* from the cashier, a stout Arab wearing a crimson fez with a black tassel that swayed in front of his black moustache.

I put the *jeton* in the gray metal box that hung on the yellow ceramic-tiled wall and tried not to breathe. The W.C. stank. I dialed, then heard the annoying beep, beep, beep.

Why did the French complicate things? Even the phone system was perverse. It was antiquated. It belonged in a museum, not on the wall at my fingertips. I missed the simplicity of Pacific Bell.

I pressed the red button which stopped that infernal beeping, guaranteed to give a migraine, and was able to hear Chanda's "*Allô?*"

"Well, if it isn't the sexpot!" she said breathing heavily. "I wish my film had gotten so much attention. *Chérie*, it's all over *Paris Match*, every magazine cover and every *affiche*. You have much to be proud of. Jean-Paul, will he agree? He's such a—how you say—prod, prude? Ta ta. You want Grams?" Chanda passed the phone to *grand-mère*.

"*Allô.*"

"Grams, have you seen it?" I asked, holding my nose. A man

still zipping his fly walked out of the W.C., leaving the door ajar. (A dirty American bathroom never smelled as bad as a dirty French bathroom.)

"*Oui, oui, mon enfant*, eet is verry verry goood. Do not be ashamed. Never be ashamed of the beautiful body God gave you."

"*Merci*, Grams. What does Laurence say?"

"*La même chose.*"

"Will Jean-Paul be angry?"

"You are underestimating my grandson. But Jean-Paul will react as Jean-Paul reacts. *Voilà!* I am here for you as well as him."

"*Merci*, Grams. You always make me feel better."

"Ah, but it is you who have made yourself feel better."

I hung up wondering why everyone in the whole wide world wasn't as loving as Grams. Most of all, why wasn't I?

Then I quickly walked back into the restaurant and waved "Ta ta!" to the gloating Arab, still twirling his moustache as he studied my exit.

Walking up the Champs-Elysées wearing a white polyester uniform, white sponge-soled shoes, a blond wig and a bandanna and feeling like a star. What fun! No one noticed me. No! I noticed me. Even the sun was trying to push its rays through stubborn black cumulus clouds with "I Love Paris" embossed on them. I imagined L'Etoile in sunlight surrounded by palm trees and transported to the busy intersection across from the Beverly Hills Hotel on Sunset Boulevard.

When I reached a newsstand, I looked back down the Champs-Elysées and saw the long queue for the next showing, my name over my naked body floating atop the theater's marquee.

I scanned the newsstand. *Jour de France, Pariscope, Marie Claire* and *Elle* had photos of me and Super T. on their covers. After buying a copy of each, I hailed a cab. Jean-Paul would call tonight and then I would see Sacha.

When I opened the door, I felt a *squoosh!* Something smelled.

Tutu, not greeting me enthusiastically as usual, sat on the opposite side of the foyer. Why, he had done his poos right in front of
the door. Goodness, he hadn't done that for years. He was
pissed off because I hadn't taken him to see *The Starlet*. It was
the maid's day off (thank God I was wearing her shoes!). I
quickly cleaned up the mess without scolding him. Instead I
showed him our magazine covers. Once he saw how famous we
were, he apologized by licking my face. Repeatedly.

The phone rang.

"Hey, Ms. Starlet, the audience couldn't stop jabbering about
you."

"What did they say?"

"How should I know? I left my translator at the U.N. The
men wolf-whistled and looked excited and the women looked
jealous. The perfect combo for word of mouth."

"If you say so."

"What are you doing tonight, Ms. Bare Ass?"

"Cleaning the dog shit off the maid's shoes, for one thing,
waiting for Jean-Paul to call, then having sex with Sacha."

"Sounds like a big night. Well, hoped we could hit a male
strip club or some kinky after-hours joint."

"Another night, Z. My emotions are playing roulette."

"I'll hang on whatever that means. Sweet dreams, Ms. Movie
Queen."

Tutu and I enjoyed a low-cal snack while I read my interviews to him. Who said looking at your own publicity wasn't
fun?

At nine o'clock Jean-Paul called.

"Can't tell you, Maya, when I've ever sat in a movie theater
wanting to make love to the star when I already have. I underes-
timated your talent."

"Oh, Jean-Paul, I was so afraid of what you'd think."

"We'll talk about your career tomorrow. I'll be on the three
o'clock flight from Fumicino."

"How's Rome?"

"Maybe you'll come with me next week and see for yourself?"

When he hung up, I felt so close to Jean-Paul. How could I go running off to Sacha? My confusion lasted sixty seconds.

Sacha had seen *The Starlet* early in the evening and apologized for not casting me in Darian Nelson's role in his film. "My dear, I wonder if you will ever forgive me?" he asked.

I wondered myself. "I would like to have been offered the part, but you know Jean-Paul wouldn't have allowed me to do it." My career was just beginning. I had two men in love with me and was worthy of them both. As I took a cab home late that night, I thought how lucky I was. Why, I had everything!

In the morning I was awakened as usual by the peculiar honklike ring of the telephone. Even the phone had an accent.

"Maya?" It was Z. She never called me by my name.

"Good morning," I said, eager to comfort her.

"Not so good." Her voice was high and strained.

"What's not so good?"

"The English papers."

"What English papers?"

"Fleet Street tabloids."

"You read that dreck?"

"Yep, me and millions of other gossip-starved housewives."

"So?"

"So, you're the headlines."

"Great."

"Not so great."

"More PR, the better it is for the film."

"This is not about the film."

"What?"

"Sit down and pour yourself a long stiff one. Do you know a black guy who worked at Carte Blanche Liquors?"

I didn't respond.

"Seems he sold a story about you to *News of the World*."

"Excuse me, Z. I'm getting that drink."

I dropped the receiver and shuffled in my fluffy bedroom slippers to the kitchen. The maid was out shopping. Thank God. Sitting on a high stool close to the ice, orange juice and vodka, I picked up the receiver of the wall phone.

"So what did he say?" I asked.

"A lot. Is it true?"

"WHAT DID HE SAY?" I shouted.

"Easy, girl, easy. It's not bad press really! Once you recover from the shock. I've already talked to Eric in Holly—"

"YOU TOLD HIM?" I screamed.

"Told him? He called me. It's all over the trades and on T.V."

"What am I going to do?"

"Frankly, Maya, it really is very kinky and—"

"Kinky! You call jerking off in front of a delivery guy kinky?"

"Yeah! Look, see Evelyn. Thank God you're in France. Those frogs won't even think twice. They're so wonderfully perverse . . . they'll love you. Just accept it!"

"Accept being exposed as an exhibitionist? You crazy?"

"You're bare-ass naked in the film and kinky there. What's the dif? See Evelyn. Then take a Valium."

"What will Jean-Paul say?" I cried.

"For the last time, see Evelyn. I love you. Call me anytime."

Click!

I downed my vodka.

I called Evelyn. Tutu tried to lick away my tears. No answer. Therapists! Never there when you needed them.

I took three Valiums, downed them with vodka and passed out. At 4 P.M. the maid woke me to say she was leaving and had prepared *lapin* for Jean-Paul. We were going to have a romantic candlelit dinner. Were.

He would be home in an hour. I made some coffee and began dressing. If I looked beautiful, maybe he'd be less angry. I could manipulate him. Oh, hell! There was no way he was going to accept this. What if all those other men were to sell their stories too? Could I be arrested? Would Jean-Paul commit me? Divorce me, yes. But would he commit me? I had to be insane. How could I ever return to Hollywood? They laughed at any kind of sexual aberration and waited for gossip like this to burn up their phone lines.

Sacha should be back from the set. I dialed. No answer. Damn! I left a message with the greengrocer. Sacha would hear the news as Z had. In fact, why hadn't he called? He knew Jean-Paul was out of town. Sacha was dumping me too! My stories were OK in private, but public knowledge about Maya Endicott flashing her pubes would disgust him. Miss Lily White Candice would never do anything like that.

I heard a key in the door. Tutu wagged his stub of a tail. I inhaled deeply and tried to smile. The corners of my mouth felt as if they had been stapled to my chin.

"How was Rome, *chéri*?" I asked as the door opened.

Jean-Paul's face was contorted. His nostrils flared. He waved a newspaper clenched in his fist. "Don't *chéri* me, Mrs. Flasher!" His voice crackled and his top lip curled up in a sneer. He gritted his teeth. His eyes looked like black holes. "How many besides this black dude are there?"

"Jean-Paul, I'm sorry. I don't know why I did it," I cried, trying to put my arms around him.

He pushed me away. "You're a pervert. That's why!"

"You're unfair."

"My wife offering pubic inspection to every delivery boy is fair?"

"I want to go to a hospital. Something's wrong with me."

"You're telling me? Go to a hospital after you move your things out of my life."

"Please help me?"

"Help yourself. You want to be a beaver queen. Be it on your own time."

"You'll never be more than your father's son."

Jean-Paul grabbed my elbow with one hand and hit me with the other.

"Let go."

"Apologize!"

"What for?"

He slapped me again. "For being a fuckin' pervert."

"Kill me. Then you'll be somebody."

He pushed me onto the floor. He rubbed my face against the carpet. "Say you're sorry, c-cunt!"

"I'm sorry I married you."

He pounded my head on the bedpost.

"I'm sorry I know you."

He kicked me in the ribs.

"S-Say it!"

"*It!*" I shouted.

Tutu ran in between us. He kicked him. I heard a sharp cry. Now I was afraid for Tutu. I said, "I'm sorry."

Jean-Paul released me. The door slammed. I placed Tutu by the side of the bed. He was whimpering and didn't move. I popped two Quaaludes with white wine and passed out. I hoped I wouldn't wake up.

But I did. I smelled a foul odor. Rot. Gas. I reached for Tutu. His eyes were closed. He felt like stone. He was dead. I held him as I went into the bathroom for my bottle of Valium. What would do it? There were fifteen left. Enough. With a pair of scissors I cut off a lock of his brown curly coat and put it under my pillow. Then I crawled into bed, holding him on top of my belly. We said our prayers. I knew he heard me. I heard him. And then we fell back to sleep.

16

THE detoxification program at the American Hospital wasn't for a movie queen: up at seven, make my bed, empty the trash, breakfast, group therapy, psychodrama, lunch, drug and alcohol group, independent living skills, aerobics, issues of adulthood independence, handicrafts (basket-weaving).

Laurence, along with Evelyn, had committed me the morning after I'd taken the pills. Sacha visited, and Jean-Paul brought flowers, presents and apologies.

I informed Evelyn when she signed the commitment papers that I wasn't an alcoholic or an addict or an exhibitionist. My attempted suicide was because of Tutu's death.

"And those bruises?" she said.

I laughed. "I asked Jean-Paul to kill me."

She didn't laugh.

The second day Z called. "What's with the overacting? I said take *one* Valium!"

My doctors said my problem was that I didn't know how to deal with my feelings because I didn't feel I had a right to them. Therefore I had repressed my anger. I would have to talk and write about anything, any secrets—everything—that made me angry. They made me angry. I stalled and stalled. I suspected they wanted me to write about my flashing. Jean-Paul had probably ratted. The horny staff wanted to get their rocks off. I lost every pen they gave me and claimed I was allergic to graphite.

Finally the men and women in white coats began hounding

me about what made me the most angry. "Doctors!" I shouted. "Those lousy scumbags who drilled holes in my father's brain!"

That shut the white jackets up for a while. But then they came back all smiles and sweetness and told me the sooner I wrote about my feelings, and my flashing (they were on to me), the sooner I would get out of that hellhole.

I pulled aside a doctor who wore a crew cut, thick tortoise-shell glasses and no smile. "Look, doc, let's get honest. You and the rest of your crew just want to get off on my lewd behavior."

Calmly, always calmly, the doctor replied, "Ms. Endicott, your behavior was lewd, but not that lewd. And in all honesty, you're pretty, but not that pretty. However, your sense of importance—ego—is massive. Frankly we, the staff, don't care what you've done. We don't care that you're a so-called movie star. To us you're just another drunk and addict. We have a job to do and patients who want our help. The sooner you cooperate, the sooner you will get well and get out of here. Now if you'll excuse me. My time is valuable."

The next day I lost my allergy to graphite and pulled out twenty pens I had stashed around my cell. Four hundred pages later, with all my flashing tales committed to a yellow memo pad, I felt lighter, different—and, I hated to admit, better. I had cried a lot. Thank God no one had seen me. I read what I had written to the doctors, who didn't laugh or react.

I had to call Z! She'd be proud of me.

"Hey, Z, it's Camille."

She laughed, happy to hear my voice. "You sound pretty lively for a corpse trainee."

"This joint's hard work. I wrote down all my flashing stories and told them to the doctors, who said Mom's forcing that plastic nozzle into me was a form of sodomy, but she didn't realize what she was doing."

"Ye gads, woman, no wonder you're so angry! What *I* want to know is how many guys were there, and what did you do to them? I want lessons. Life's dull. Can't I be your apprentice? Assistant? Dresser?"

"Stop it, Z." I laughed. "It's humiliating."

"To you. To me it's funny. Kinky. I'm envious. So little and so few turn me on."

"Oh, I guess it's funny when I think back."

"How about thinking forward? Tell me how you plan it. Set it up?"

"Cut it out, Z. I just called to tell you I'm talking about it, and they say that means I'm getting better."

"Hey, Ms. Perfect Bod, you always were better. That's why I've been jealous."

"Oh, Z, I miss you. Why don't you come in here with me?"

"What?"

"Stop your pill habit?"

"Hey, don't pull a Carrie Nation with me. I have my pill-taking under control. And don't tell those straight arrows that I forged prescriptions to get you those pills or I'll be looking at life behind bars."

"I'd never rat on you. Oops, gotta go. Lights out. It's ten o'clock."

"You're going to bed? I'm going to dinner! Get out soon. Gotta go back to L.A. in a month. I'm losing my tan!"

I smiled and thought I would do what the doctors said just to be with Z.

After four weeks of talk, talk and more talk, I was released, feeling like an infant with a handicap. The doctors told me my stay in the hospital was just a beginning. They called recovery a process, a way of life. Behind their backs, I yawned. They said my character had to grow or my spirit would wither. Was that why I had wanted to die?

For six weeks I hadn't drunk or used drugs, and no matter how much I had hated the rules, the digging up of the pain of the past, when I left the American Hospital I felt terrific!

Everything seemed new. Colors were vivid. I noticed the mortar between bricks, seams in cobblestones, license plates, numbers, ripples in the Seine. How wonderful to be in Paris on a cloudy day!

When I looked in the mirror, I no longer saw that puffy face. I needed less makeup, even no makeup. Every butcher, baker, cab driver did not have to see me with my eyeliner, my mascara, my lip gloss.

Jean-Paul had taken a three-week course at the same hospital in the Family Renewal Center to help him understand me and my bizarre sexual displays. I was touched. Tutu's death might haunt me, but I had to forgive Jean-Paul. He might be suffering more than me. My doctors told me not to make drastic changes in my life, not these first months.

I continued to see Sacha, but my feelings for him were raw. I was trying to be honest about what I felt. I wanted that honesty from others. He was trying, but by nature he was a liar, just as I had been.

When I was released, it was suggested—like Novocain is suggested for tooth extraction—that I go to AA meetings. God, did I hate them. I went to synagogues, church basements, Hungarian clubhouses, cathedrals, banks, gymnasiums, YMCA's. All kinds of people—types I ran from all my life—were shoved into one poorly lit space to listen to each other's stories. When the meetings were over, I felt better. I couldn't explain it. I didn't try, not even to Z.

We lunched regularly, but the hoop-de-doo of four-star restaurants had lost its attraction. I preferred the charm of small bistros, little cafés.

One day we lunched at Le Petit Saint-Benoît, a sidewalk café off the Boulevard Saint-Germain. Jugglers, mime artists and an accordian player were performing in the street.

We were sitting next to a fat man with whiskers and a black toupee.

"I want to see a menu."

"I sure miss Maxim's, Ms. Outpatient!" Z said, drumming her freshly manicured nails on the table.

The fat man looked at Z and belched.

"How much longer will you be in Paris?" I asked, suppressing my laughter.

"Leaving next week. Eric is threatening to cut my vacation pay."

"It's great he's so understanding."

"Yeah, Eric's a pisser! He's got a good idea regarding your scandal. He thinks you should sell your side of your story to a newspaper."

"How could I do that?"

"How can I eat lunch here?"

"I see your point."

"Go to *Sunday People* or the *Daily Mail*. A competitor of *News of the World*. You'll get a hundred, maybe a hundred fifty thousand. Give it to charity. Tell about going to the hospital, your tragic childhood, and you'll come out smelling like a kinky saint."

"You mean, 'How I Became a Pervert' by Maya Endicott?"

"You can turn this whole thing around. That's what Harold Robbins says," Z said, smiling as though she were entering the Pearly Gates.

"That's such a risk!"

"Yep. Risks are great, Ms. Chastity Mind. Loosen up. Fly light. If you ever want to come back to L.A., this is the way!"

"They'd stone me there."

"Not if you put your heart on the page and seal it with the press. Don't underestimate old H'wood. There're some decent folks. You gotta reach out to them. The assholes are just noisier."

I said, "I'll think about it."

I thought about it—how the doctors had wanted me to write about my shame. I had nothing to lose but fear—a good reason to do it.

The next day I began writing, and by the end of the week Michael Stone had sold my story to London's *Daily Mail* for

$200,000. The money was donated to Dr. Patrick Carnes, author of *The Sexual Addiction*, for his treatment center in Minneapolis, Minnesota. Recovering sex addicts at the hospital studied his text.

I had done all I could do. I was emotionally wrung out, not in the mood to go anywhere, least of all AA. Jean-Paul was full of concern, and Sacha was more loving than ever. Why was I sentenced to such a life? Nonetheless, I walked down the stone steps of an Episcopal church in Montmartre and followed the signs to the meeting. First I stopped in the kitchen to grab a cup of coffee and a croissant. There was always coffee. It was as smoky as usual in the lime-green neon-lit cellar. I put my raincoat over a vacant chair and sat in the last row. I was late as usual. The speaker had already begun. Another sob story. A woman. God, was I sick of everyone trying to out-suffer everyone else.

"His philandering is his business. Because of my belief in a higher power, I never feel abandoned or alone."

I thought, This one's in real trouble.

"When we lived in Hollywood..."

Hollywood?

"...there was a different starlet every night."

Her voice sounded familiar. I had forgotten my glasses. I began to squint to see her face.

"He still sees her today, but I accept his need to have more than one woman. That's part of who he is. I come to these meetings to learn how to accept others, not to change them."

It was Candice! No wonder she had always seemed so serene! These meetings would turn anyone into a zombie. So this is how she tolerates Sacha's shenanigans. Amazing!

"Today, I try to allow him the dignity to lead his life his way, and try not to blame anyone for my behavior anymore. So by the grace of God I'm..." Oh, not again. I tuned out till I heard: "I now open the meeting up to a show of hands."

I was tempted to raise mine and say, "Hi, Candice!" But I

didn't dare. Could I learn to accept her as she accepted Sacha? If I could have her attitude, I could stay married to Jean-Paul, see Sacha and not feel this torment.

Oddly enough, sex with Jean-Paul had improved. He was being kind. Also, *The Starlet* was a hit. My only worry was what Sacha was doing when he wasn't with me. Could I dare talk to Candice? Or was that madness? Wouldn't she tell the AA members I was the tart trying to steal her man? But she didn't talk like that at the podium. She seemed loving. In a state of grace. That's what she had. I didn't.

Oh, what the hey. I got in line to shake hands with the speaker. I felt like I was on latrine duty. A newcomer. People with a lot of sober time had a look: a slight smile, a glow. Nothing bothered them. God, did I want to be like that.

Nervously I stood in line. My turn. "Thank you, Candice," I heard myself say.

"Maya, how good to see you. Here." She held my cold hand between her palms and wouldn't let go. I thought I was in a movie. "How are you?"

"Coping."

"Your skin looks wonderful. Clearer."

"Thanks." She meant the compliment.

"Would you like to have coffee? We should have a laugh."

"Why not?" I said.

We went to a nearby sidewalk café. The sun was setting on Sacré Coeur. I couldn't believe this was happening.

Candice began. "I heard about your hospital stay from Jean-Paul. I was going to visit, but I thought I'd wait for the higher powers to take over."

I couldn't tell if she was serious or not. "How long have you been in AA?" I asked.

"Fifteen years." (Unbelievable, I thought.) "I'm speaking again next week, if you want to hear my whole story. I noticed you came in at the end . . ."

I didn't listen to her rhetoric. Instead I watched and felt her calm, then thought I might as well stick a pin into all that hot air. "Doesn't it bother you that I'm having an affair with Sacha?"

She didn't flinch, but smiled on. "I've stopped looking for unconditional love in anyone. That's not human. Only God can give me that." (All this God talk was making my head spin.) "You see, I can't feel someone's feelings, but I am able to feel my love for them. That's the gift. I'd rather feel love than be loved. Sacha and I are free in spirit. So our relationship has lasted."

Should I tell her I know she's having an affair with Jean-Paul? "I don't think Sacha or Jean-Paul should know we've met here, do you?"

"No reason for them to. It's none of their business. This meeting's for ladies only!"

"Does Sacha know you come to meetings?"

"Men don't need to know everything. Only to think they do."

Suddenly I saw why Jean-Paul and Sacha liked Candice. I liked her too. "Well, I won't tell Sacha, either." (But wait till I tell Z!) I extended my hand. "Shake?"

"Good."

"I must say I was jealous."

"You needn't have been. If women were less jealous of one another, men would have less power over us."

That night Jean-Paul asked me how the meeting went. I replied with a Mona Lisa grin, the one I spotted on Candice, "Boring as usual." Then I excused myself to telephone Z, who was leaving in the morning.

"You'll never guess who I met in a meeting, Zoe."

"Thought AA was anonymous."

"You don't count!"

"Thanks!"

"You're family. C'mon."

"Nancy Reagan?"

"Candice McIlhenney!"

"No shit. So that's why she's such a snore!" Z inhaled through her nose, making a grunting sound.

"Z, she's nice and she's not a bore. She's my friend."

"Are you premenstrual?"

"Honest! She's terrific!"

"Now she'll tell Sacha and play all sorts of games. You've had your hot rollers on your head too long."

"Listen, she's great. She promised not to tell. So did I."

"I hope her word's better than yours."

"It is. She's fifteen years sober."

"Dear God. There is life after drugs! Look, Miss Dummkopf, if it makes you happy to pal around with your lover's main squeeze, do it. But be careful! Isn't she still banging Jean-Paul?"

"We haven't got there yet."

"What do you mean, 'we'?"

"I'm waiting for her to want to tell me. But I've told her I love Sacha."

"You do need a brain scan!"

"I trust her, Z."

"The Germans trusted Hitler."

"You'll see. Don't worry."

"How can I not worry? I tell you to take one Valium, you take fifteen. Now you tell Candice that you're screwing her guy and she's not telling you that she's screwing your guy. You dames are unreal. Look, gotta hang. I'll call you from L.A. When I take my Valium, I'll think of you."

I told Jean-Paul I was off to acting class and went to see Sacha.

The door to his suite was unlocked, the curtains drawn. I walked into the bedroom. It smelled like an infirmary. Bottles of pills were opened, caps strewn on top of a table within his reach. In a corner a humidifier emitted a vapor with a medicinal odor. A haggard Sacha lay in bed wearing long underwear and a maroon flannel robe. I'd never seen him looking so old. "Come by my side, my pet," he said wearily.

I began to undress.

"No, no, stay as you are."

"I don't understand," I said sitting on the edge of the bed clutching the sheet.

"Not to fret, precious. It's only flu."

"You gave me a scare," I sighed. I curled under the covers and held his perspiring body.

"Cuddle up against me, my darling. I've written a poem I want you to listen to," he said as though he were about to read the Ten Commandments.

> To Maya
> Bird, angel, hoyden, shrew,
> Witch, bitch through and through,
> Sport, spirit, flasher, sprite,
> Some good man's going to treat you right!

I wasn't going to ask who the good man was. What a terrible poem! "Why, that's lovely, Sacha," I said, smiling.

"Thank you, Maya. Now, in exchange, why don't you tell me one of your flashing tales to take my mind off these silly chest pains?" Gently he patted my back.

"But that excites you," I said.

"My darling, I only have the flu. And you know your doctors told you to talk about it."

"To them," I said like a guilty three-year-old. I no longer wanted to play this game, but I couldn't say no to Sacha—yet. "I'll do anything to make you feel better, but why do you like to listen to what I've done with other men—especially something so tacky?"

"Ah, it makes me feel young, when I was daring, reckless, carefree. I envy your free spirit, my dear. Whether it's yours or something that possesses you, it's rebelling against conformity. I respect that."

Sacha hated his own attitudes—but not enough to change them. No wonder hearing about my perversities excited him.

"My darling, pretend I'm your doctor."

"Yes, let's play doctor." I clasped his hands, now holding my waist, and pretended I was a patient visiting a therapist. The eyelet trim on the pillow case became the focus of my attention. Clutching the pillow, I talked to the eyelet's delicate design. "I was sitting by the pool of the Hotel Carlisle in Cannes. It was late in the day and the place was deserted. The palm trees hid the pool from the hotel. A single attendant was waiting for me to return my towel. I lay topless on the chaise longue and felt him staring at me. I spread my legs."

"Hold me, Maya." Sacha put my hand between his legs. "What did he look like?"

"Short, with a stubby beard, white hair, black eyes. A long scar from one eye to his ear. Thin lips. Italian. He wore a faded red uniform with those phony gold epaulets on each shoulder. He grinned. I signaled as though I wanted a drink, then loosened my string bikini so that it fell away from my body. I was covered in suntan oil. I began to rub more on. Between my legs. He came closer. He was now a few feet away. He stood there looking between my legs."

"Ah, what pleasure you gave the poor man. Stroke me. Continue," Sacha said weakly.

"I pretended I didn't know what was happening. I was in a trance. Hot. Nothing frightens me when I'm hot. I was leading Mr. Rome."

"I like that . . . Mr. Rome." Sacha chuckled. "The conquest of Signor Roma. Go on, my darling."

"I rubbed myself with more suntan oil and said, 'There's a screw loose under this thing.'"

Sacha laughed, coughing up phlegm.

"I don't think this is good for you."

"Never mind," Sacha said, growling. "Let me be the judge of that."

"Mr. Rome was looking at my nakedness."

"Your pussy. Your big black pussy!" Sacha said. Where had he got his energy? I was holding it. He had been listening with his penis. "Go on. Go on."

"'What do you want, lady?' Mr. Rome asked. I stood up, then squatted, spread my thighs and said, 'Come here.' Mr. Rome looked down at me and hesitated."

"Why?"

"He wanted me to tell him what to do. He stooped beside me, looked under the chair, then between my legs. He fiddled with the chair, then said, 'Lady, you need a screw.'"

"Bet you didn't argue," said Sacha, shaking with laughter. "Continue!"

"He reached for my body. I wouldn't let him touch me. I stared into his eyes, imagining he was my servant, then lay back on the concrete, spread my legs on either side of his kneeling body. He had unzipped his fly and was stroking himself."

"What did his Roman appendage look like?" Sacha smiled. His face was red, his voice groggy.

All men, even on their deathbed, want to know about other men. "His was thin, long, with white pubic hair. Now that buzzing and humming made me feel like I was floating. My mind—no longer part of my flesh—was looking down at my body and laughing. I rolled from side to side."

"And he was looking right up your snatch," said Sacha, coughing.

He looked so weak. I pulled my hand away.

"Don't stop what you've started. Trying to give me a heart attack?" He angrily shoved my hand back on his willpower, yanking it savagely.

"I was modeling my body on the bare concrete in front of Mr. Rome."

Sacha moaned. His spirit shot onto my hand.

"Finish your story, my pet." He sighed. A smile covered his unshaven face, which looked twenty years younger.

"Then I came," I said, relieved.

"He didn't insist on touching you?"

"I told him I'd report him for attempted rape if he got fresh."

"If he got fresh?" Sacha smiled. "You are mad, my love. Completely mad."

"We know that," I laughed, cleaning off his loveliness.

"You have made me feel better. What do doctors know about life?"

I looked into his face. He was glowing. His eyes were bright. Color had come back into his cheeks. He stroked my hair in a fatherly way and smiled. The gentleman, Dr. Jekyll, had returned; Mr. Hyde, the sex maniac, had been satisfied. He held my hands, squeezed them and said, "Darling, don't ever be ashamed of who you are or who you have been."

I kissed his full tender lips, no longer pulsating with frustrated passion, then fell asleep in his arms.

I saw Sacha once a week and Candice once a week. She told me I was good for Sacha and he loved me very much. His feelings for me had nothing to do with his feelings for her. Her tolerance was baffling.

Apparently Sacha had no idea I had met Candice—a woman of her word. She had yet to confess her affair with Jean-Paul. Instead she kept pushing me to choose a God. Intrigue was my God. And orgasms. She wanted me to join a gym for my frustrated sex drive. I was more concerned with exercise in bed with Sacha and seducing him into seeing me more. He balked.

"Maya, if I don't get financing for my next film, I will be bankrupt. I know you'll think I'm using you if I ask you to try to influence Jean-Paul, but you must see my position. It is grave."

"My darling, you've never been honest with me before."

"We could all benefit. I would like to invite you and Jean-Paul to dinner with Candice and me. Brasserie Lipp?" Moments later I was enjoying his lips, his flesh. I was going to reward him for his honesty.

Whenever I left Sacha's hotel, I stopped at the corner café at Rue du Bac and St.-Germain and had a cappuccino.

What a gorgeous winter day! Sounds were crisp. Traffic, birds, silence—all were entities, magnified. Or was I just notic- ing the world because I was going to meetings and listening to people talk about themselves?

Candice was trying to make me "commit" spiritually. There clearly hadn't been a greater power anywhere around for my father. God had just sat up there and watched my father. And Tutu! How could I find—much less come to believe in—a higher power? Well, I hadn't succeeded in killing myself. What was working in my life that time?

I sipped my cappuccino and thought about Tutu. Tears fell into the saucer. Maybe Tutu had to be taken away for me to become strong like Candice. Tutu had loved me unconditionally. No one, not even Sacha, had ever given me that kind of love. Oh, hell, Sacha was human. Animals could love uncondition- ally. Like God.

I looked at a woman's gray toy poodle in front of me. Cer- tainly he didn't have the sense of humor of Tutu, or the spirit. Why didn't I think of it before? Make Tutu my God! Super- toots! He'd never liked me to drink. He would try to knock over my wine. His death might have saved my life.

When I returned to the apartment, Jean-Paul was in a great mood. It seemed like as good a moment as any. "My love, guess who I ran into on the Champs-Elysées? Sacha and Candice. We all went for cappuccino."

"Since when are you and Candice cappuccino buddies?"

"Oh, I don't have anything against her, darling, as long as she keeps her grubby little claws off you."

Jean-Paul laughed. "I told you before, she's not my type."

"Let's have tea. I want to talk to you about something."

We walked down the long corridor to the kitchen.

"Darling, Sacha wants to talk with you about a film he's putting together. He's inviting us to dinner to discuss it."

Jean-Paul began laughing. "I'll listen only because you've been trying so hard. I have to tell you I think Sacha's a lame-brain and only looking to produce women, but . . ."

"Jean-Paul, really! Lipp, this Tuesday?"

"Fine by me."

THAT night at eight o'clock I went to the AA meeting at the American Cathedral on the Avenue Georges V. Candice would be there.

Afterward we met for coffee at Le Drugstore on the Champs-Elysées.

"Candice, you'll never believe this. Sacha has invited Jean-Paul and me to have dinner with you on Tuesday!"

"What on earth for?"

"He wants Jean-Paul to back his next film."

"I know he's in trouble financially. Jean-Paul has agreed?"

"Yes, because I've been trying so hard...he says." I thought of Supertoots and hoped Candice would find the courage to tell me she was having an affair with Jean-Paul.

"Maya, I've been waiting for you to adjust to having met me before I told you this. You know how I feel about men and relationships and marriage." She was tense. That Mona Lisa smile had vanished. "I'm having an affair with Jean-Paul."

"Candice." I held her cold hand between my palms. "I know."

"You do?"

"It's OK."

"How did you know?"

"I saw you together one day before my breakdown."

"You never told me. Why?"

"I wanted you to tell me. Like you taught me, it was none of my business."

She began to smile. I was so glad to see she was real. Our relationship was becoming as important as my relationship with the men. I had never felt this close friendship with a woman before.

"Didn't Jean-Paul ever tell you that I saw you together?"

"Never a word."

"How sneaky men can be," I said, feigning contempt.

We laughed into our once-hot fudge sundaes.

What to wear? I no longer felt comfortable with my cleavage on display. If I returned to acting I would wear low-cut dresses to openings, parties, auditions. That look was business. But now I hid my body. Cleavage drew too much attention. I was learning how little attention had to do with love.

I slicked my hair back into a chignon and selected a charcoal herringbone suit and white silk shirt that Jean-Paul and Sacha liked. How agreeable to please them both. Though I loved Candice, I certainly wanted to look better than her.

Jean-Paul wore one of his monogrammed shirts and a three-piece suit. I laughed. Sacha would be wearing a three-piece suit. That was all he had.

"*Tu es mignon, chéri,*" I said, kissing Jean-Paul on the cheek. "I know you are doing this for me." (Or was he doing it for Candice?)

Passing the long queue of elegant Parisians and foreigners sipping apéritifs in the enclosed sidewalk café of Brasserie Lipp was always an event. When we entered the restaurant with its many mirrors and bright lights, every eye was on us. Jean-Paul was a celebrity, and so was I—of a different sort. The maître d', cordial but distant, led us through the conservative crowd to the best table. Sacha and Candice were already seated on the burgundy velvet banquette.

After introductions and three minutes of preliminaries, Sacha began. "Jean-Paul, I would like to produce a film in which Maya would star."

Sacha hadn't told me this.

The waiter appeared. Drinks were ordered. I hadn't thought about wine for weeks, but I did now. I ordered a Perrier, a glass of orange juice and a Coke, a trick I had learned so that I would not have to order again and face temptation.

Sacha looked so much more handsome than Jean-Paul. I sat comparing the two and pretended they were auditioning for me. Something was placed in my lap. A piece of paper. A note. When the waiter served the drinks, I looked down and read, "Meet me in the ladies' after the hors d'oeuvres."

I smiled, nodded.

"What sort of film are you proposing?" Jean-Paul said.

"Well, Maya has a great sense of comic timing. I have several projects in mind, but above all there must be no possibility of exploiting her."

"Perhaps I was wrong to ask her to q-quit acting. Apparently *The Starlet* is breaking box office records. A career may be necessary. Those AA meetings are not always enough," said Jean-Paul, sipping his wine.

"Yes, I know what you mean," Sacha said. I felt his big toe rubbing my calf, moving upward.

I let out a sound as his toe moved to my thighs. "Oh," I sighed, "I do need something to do with my time." I was holding Sacha's big toe right at my crotch. Candice, elbows on table, was staring intensely into Jean-Paul's eyes. He loosened his collar. Sacha was going to get the money after all.

Sacha ordered oysters as an appetizer. I remembered serving him oysters in bed. Slipping them into his mouth. Him eating them out of mine. Now, as he drank the juice, he looked into my eyes. I took off my jacket, hoping to avoid his gaze.

"Maya, would you like a taste?" he said. I opened my mouth and closed my eyes. I didn't have the nerve to look at him. As he laid the oyster on my tongue, I thought of his flesh. When I opened my eyes, Sacha was looking businesslike at Jean-Paul while thrusting his toe further into my crotch.

I made a noise. "Oh, the oysters are delicious."

"Aren't they?" Candice said, looking into Jean-Paul's eyes. He hadn't caught on. Or he didn't care.

After the first course, Candice and I left for the ladies' room, thrusting our noses in the air as we walked somberly away. Once inside we laughed until our mascara covered our cheeks.

"Candice, it's working. Jean-Paul loves the idea."

"How are you feeling?"

"Good."

"If you feel like drinking, pinch my thigh and I'll meet you here. Otherwise back here at coffee?"

"Are we mad, Candice? Why am I not with Sacha, and you with Jean-Paul?"

"Dear, all men want a mistress. We must keep their philandering in the family. Safe within the family." She grinned. "Leave me behind in the ladies' room. That's the rude thing to do."

When I sat down at the table, Jean-Paul said as though I had been rude, "Where's Candice?"

"She'll be along," I said with a smile.

Sacha smiled.

Moments later Candice arrived, and we all smiled.

The waiter displayed the sole Jean-Paul and I had ordered. Sacha said, "I think the best property I have is a modern-day version of a Feydeau farce. Don't you like that one, Candice?"

"Yes, but *Tartuffe* isn't bad either."

"Ah, yes, that is Candice's favorite."

"I'm quite fond of Molière as well," Jean-Paul said, looking into Candice's eyes.

"Are you? I didn't know," she said.

"Candice is very opinionated when it comes to the classics," Sacha said. "What about Giraudoux?"

I didn't know what they were talking about. I hadn't read Feydeau or Molière or Giraudoux. Candice was off in another world with them and I wasn't part of it. I imagined a bone in my throat and began to cough. I wasn't well read, but I could act. "Oh, please excuse me," I said, jumping up from the table. Then I quickly walked to the back of the restaurant and mounted the spiral stairs to a small bar.

"Gin and tonic, please." I felt a hand on my waist. It was Candice.

"You were to pinch me on the thigh."

"Don't pretend, Candice."

"Feeling left out?"

The gin and tonic was placed on the bar.

"What do you think?" I held the drink in my hand.

"You think that is going to make you more cultured?"

I put the glass to my lips. "Listen, Candice, at least I won't have to feel this hole in my gut."

"Jealousy, you mean?"

"I'm not jealous of you. And it's not the books . . ."

"It's the attention."

"Right."

"To get attention you have to give it. Do you mind if someone else has the spotlight for a moment? This entire dinner is for your benefit. To star in a movie. The first part of the dinner I didn't say more than one word. Just because I happen to have read three plays you haven't, you feel left out."

I smiled. "They were both nice to you and forgot about me."

"Have more trust. The feelings they have for you aren't the same feelings they have for me. Not better, not worse, just different. They care about both of us. Accept this, or you won't stay sober."

I put the gin and tonic down. Tears fell on my cocktail napkin. "Where's a ladies'?"

She held my hand and led me to a small W.C. in the back. My mascara was again a mess. "Here's my makeup," she said, hand-ing me her handbag as she went into a toilet.

"Damn!" she shouted.

"Period?"

"Goddamn yeast infection. I've been fighting it for months."

"So have I." Seconds later we were laughing. "To cure it we're going to have to go on strike the same week." We walked down the stairs still laughing, but as we approached the table we feigned despair.

"What happened to you women?" Jean-Paul asked, sweet and rosy-cheeked from the wine.

"Maya had a coughing spell."

"Are you all right, Maya?" Sacha asked, holding my hand as I sat down.

"Fine. Really. They didn't filet the fish well."

"Funny," Jean-Paul said. "Mine was perfect."

The next day I went to the library and withdrew all the available works by Molière, Feydeau and Giraudoux.

For the next few days I plowed through them all. One night when Jean-Paul and I were reading in bed, I asked, "How do you feel about a screenplay of Molière's *Don Juan* written from a woman's point of view—*Donna Juan*?"

"Too cute! And it's been done, but I like the idea."

"What about Giraudoux's *Tiger at the Gates*?"

"More sympathetic. Helen of Troy is a terrific role for you. If you can get Jane Webb to write either screenplay, I'll finance the film completely. Tell that to your Russian playboy producer."

"Oh, Jean-Paul, how wonderful!" I embraced him. "Do you mind if I call Sacha now?"

"Why should I mind?"

I excused myself, went into the den and closed the door. Sacha was thrilled with the news. "Darling, what do you think of a film titled *Donna Juan*?"

"Too cute, sounds like a porno, but I like the idea." (Were

Sacha and Jean-Paul comparing notes?) "It should be done in L.A. A sexy movie queen who murders to become successful and delights in exploiting men," Sacha said, lowering his husky voice.

"Great. Role reversal."

"When her crime is discovered, she is imprisoned for life."

"Doesn't sound like a comedy."

"It could have its moments. You could be a twentieth-century libertine with cold, calculated sensuality who enjoys chance encounters and examines the eyes and teeth of men as though they were slaves up for auction."

"Like you do to actresses when you audition them?"

"I'm not a Don Juan."

"I've seen your address book."

"We're discussing Molière, my pet." Sacha cleared his throat. "Not your devious ways. You would have to charm every man, but not be moved yourself in any serious entanglement."

"I could use the memories of flashing."

"Absolutely. She would die a prisoner of her own state of mind."

"Make her a junkie."

"It's possible. What's your other idea?"

"Giraudoux's *Tiger at the Gates.*"

"Ah, magnificent. Make the Trojan War nuclear war. Excellent, excellent. The insanity of war. And you could be Helen of Hollywood." He chuckled.

"Too cute, Sacha."

"Well, some contemporary heroine. I'll ring Jane Webb in the morning, then take a meeting with Jean-Paul. My love, you've done it again."

"For us," I whispered, blowing a kiss into the phone.

One day when Jean-Paul was at the lawyers', Candice called to ask if she could stop by.

"I have three surprises, Maya," she said. Her voice was strained.

When I opened the door, she was seated on top of a large heavy case with a red scarf draped over it. I heard movement. "Maya, I have brought you a family."

Someone meowed.

"Two cats who were about to be killed. The mom and her two-month-old son." Candice lifted the cover over the container, opened the door and a big black and silver tabby howled and crept out onto the Oriental carpet. A black fur ball waddled out after his mom.

"Oh, Candice, they're perfect. Just what I needed."

"I know."

"I'll call them Candy and Jean-Paul Junior." I held J.P. II and hid my tears in his furry mass. "What's the third surprise?"

"Please sit down." Suddenly she was tense.

"Don't be silly."

Her face lost its color. "I'm pregnant."

"How wonderful. I will sit down." We moved into the living room and sat on the brown leather sofa. "By whom?" I asked with a quavering smile.

"Jean-Paul, of course. Sacha and I haven't had sex since we came to Paris."

I would now have a reason to divorce. God at work. "I better be godmother!"

"What are we going to do?" Candice asked, still uncomfortable.

"What do you mean, 'we'? What does he say?"

"He doesn't know."

"What?"

"If you object, Maya, I'll have an abortion."

"I'm not the father!"

"No, you're my friend."

"Candice, are you all right?"

"Of course. I've never felt better, except for occasional morning sickness. Maya, I'm thirty-eight. I was told I couldn't have children. An abortion isn't terrible. If you want to stay with Jean-Paul, I won't tell him. But if you want to go back to Hollywood, this might be your way out. The choice is yours."

I was stunned by her loyalty to me, but then realized my amazement was an insult.

"Does Sacha know?"

"No." Candy jumped on my lap and began to purr. J.P. II was inspecting the furniture. "I want the men to be free to do what they feel is right as well. How should we handle this? Suddenly you look sad."

"I would want a settlement, a fair one."

"Maya, he'd give you whatever you want. He'd have to."

"But do you think Sacha would want to be with me?"

"Of course. He'd be ecstatic."

"We have to make them think what we want is their idea," I said, grinning.

"What a good idea," Candice said, sounding relieved. "But how?"

That night Jean-Paul was horrified with the two new purring additions. He hated cats. He also hated it when I said, "Candice is pregnant. Isn't that wonderful?"

"Maya, I f-forgot something at the *boulangerie*. I'll be back shortly." Jean-Paul was white-faced as he left the apartment.

I hotfooted it to the telephone.

"What will I say?" Candice asked.

"Listen. He loves you. Don't fret. We'll talk tomorrow. Meet you at the Café Flore at ten A.M." J.P. II sat on my head and purred us to sleep. I wasn't going to wait for Jean-Paul to return and I wasn't going to tell Sacha. That was Candice's duty.

The next morning Jean-Paul was up and out of the apartment before I awakened. He had tossed and turned all night between sneezes, allergic to cats and unplanned pregnancies.

The phone was ringing, but I was too tired to answer it. I felt warmth on my face and pushed my eyelids open with both thumbs. Sun streamed through the long vertical windows, which Jean-Paul had opened. No umbrella with breakfast! *Mon dieu*, it was nine thirty! Quickly I threw on jeans, a T-shirt, a bandanna and dark glasses. Candy and J.P. II did figure eights between my legs, waving their tails like magic wands, meowing and squawking until I fed them. Then I grabbed a cab to the Café Flore. In the sunlight the bright reds, blues and greens over the tiny storefronts reminded me of a carnival, just come to town. Pity Saint-Germain-des-Prés wasn't lined with palm trees. The Café Flore was crowded.

There was Candice in gray slacks and blazer, her hair neatly arranged in a chignon, glowing like an expectant mother should glow. After kissing both her cheeks, I pulled back the cream-colored wicker chair, sat at the tiny round marble-topped table and signaled to the waiter for a *café crème*. "So?" I asked, fiddling with my bandanna.

She hesitated. Even her pause was pregnant. "Jean-Paul was all upset and said, 'How could you tell Maya first!' I said, 'Maya and I are good friends; my loyalty is to her. I don't want my pregnancy to ruin our friendship, nor do I want to be a burden to you, Jean-Paul.' He was furious. 'But I am the father,' he shouted. 'Then do something about it,' I said. 'Will you be my wife?' he said. 'I'd love to be,' I said, 'but you are married.' Suddenly we both laughed. Then I told him you wanted to return to Hollywood, but didn't mention anything about your feelings for Sacha."

"Good," I said. "What happened with Sacha?"

"He will be calling you," Candice said with a smile, sipping her *citron pressé*.

"The phone was ringing all morning. I forgot to check the messages. So what did he say?"

"He was happy for me. He's tired of the charade. Your plan was brilliant."

"Harold Robbins," I said, laughing, thinking of Z. "I'm so happy. I'll miss you, but I can't wait to get out of this town. Nothing about me's French. Here, I feel like a pregnant elephant at a fashion show," I said, dipping my baguette into my cup of coffee.

"You must think I'm a terrible hypocrite after all the things I've said against marriage."

"No, I think you're human."

"A child doesn't do well without a father."

"Don't explain, but do get married ... soon. I want to be a bridesmaid and give you away."

That night Sacha called. He was thrilled we'd be going back to L.A. and could get on with our movie without any problems.

"Darling, this is the best for all concerned," he said, though I could feel his ego had been damaged. Candice had been a weapon he had used to avoid the intimacy he feared. "You know I love you, but you and I have serious work ahead of us. Good news from Jane Webb."

"Yes? Which idea did she prefer?"

"*Tiger at the Gates*. No question. Then I spoke with Jean-Paul this afternoon and all will be arranged."

No doubt, I thought. Expectant father Jean-Paul had lost his power to negotiate. I could tell Sacha did not want to commit to me and I was relieved. My obsession for him was fading. I had never been a star and I had never been sober when I lived alone.

One month later Sacha, Candy, J.P. II and I flew out of Paris. I would miss Candice.

IT is a hot day for the first week of March—eighty-six degrees in Beverly Hills, where Sacha is doing preproduction on *Tiger at the Gates*, and ninety degrees in the valley, where I am memorizing lines in my new home in Studio City.

The phone rings.

"How's the Oscar nominee?" says Z.

"Bowled over. I can't believe that a movie like *The Starlet* would be honored by the Academy."

"It's not the movie that got the nomination, sweetpea, it's you! Want the gossip?"

"But of course. Only you would know at ten A.M. why I was nominated at six A.M."

"They don't call me the Mouth of the World for nothin'. Apparently when your blackmailer sold his story to that Fleet Street rag, your flashing tales turned on the male members of the Academy and won their votes, but created quite a scandal among the women."

"No kiddin'."

"Then, when you wrote your side of *l'histoire* you won the sympathy of the women in the Academy. Honey, you ain't the only female flasher in H'wood. June Anthony told me her phone's been ringing all morning with women too ashamed to admit it. Your story will be her next potboiler, unless you nab it first."

"Hey, I'm an actress and happy to be. I never dreamed the conservative Academy would get behind me."

"One can never be too kinky for H'wood, hot puss. What I want to know is—are you still getting the urge?"

"The urge?"

"To flash?"

"Heavens, no!"

"Not even when you visited Mom?"

"Not even when I visited Mom. I didn't have one tiny tingle."

"Drats! Kind of sorry you're cured, Ms. Sex Addict. How's it going with the Cossack? Bet Sacha misses those tales at beddy bye."

"Not as much as he misses me, I hope. Living apart is good for our relationship. Last time he went down on me I noticed bald spots."

"Oh, dear, I see what you mean."

"I never noticed them before... or cared. All his manipulation is harder for me to accept than I want to admit. So I notice his bald spots. I still love him, but I want my space. He can have his monkey business, and I won't have to know about it. There's so much I want to see and do on my own."

"Yeah, like eating at carbohydrate city, Bob's Big Boy, with all those hard hats and senior citizens? Or waiting in line for those crisp, plump chickens to come out of the ovens at Hughes's, the supermarket where you can get killed in the parking lot? Or gaping like a voyeur at the fresh veggies at Quinn's with all those health food junkies? Hey, I've been reading the copy you've been feedin' the tabloids."

"Look, I'm tired of living my life around being 'in.' *I'm* 'in.' So I like simple, honest places that are real."

"Next thing you'll be clipping coupons."

"If I weren't so impatient, I would. There's nothing wrong with respecting the value of money... even when you have it."

"Hope you're not gettin' weird on me, Ms. Perfect."

"Hey, Z, aren't you glad I'm home?"

"I suppose so. I'm just not sure if it's you or some Stepford Wife imitation. I kinda miss the girl who used to hang at the Hollywood Hills Hotel. Anyway I called to invite you to a party next Friday. Artie Gold's. You know he's producing the sequel to *Gone With the Wind*?"

"That's ridiculous!"

"Artie's ridiculous. But Sherman Elliot's directing. Windermere Studios's producing. So, Ms. Sarcasm, let's keep our laughter on low?"

"Read the script?"

"Nimble Nuts Eric pinched a copy from a secretary at Willy Morris's. It's terrific. You, Ms. Gone-Today-Here-Tomorrow, are Scarlett. I'll Xerox you a copy."

"Great. Artie's such a sleaze."

"He's a producer! Have some compassion for Hollywood's lower companions. Scuzzballs have to look in mirrors too, you know."

"But I'm busy with *Tiger at the Gates* and my agent says I have offers for the next three years."

"Offers, schmoffers. Didn't you ever dream of being boffed by Rhett Butler?"

"Yes, Mammy. Friday. Oh, Sacha's out of town raising money."

"Bet that's not all he's raising."

"Nine o'clock? I'll do my best to look like Scarlett," I say with a thick southern accent. "Before the war."

"Yes, Ms. Flasher."

When I hang up, I realize I am going to need AA before this Do Do. In Los Angeles the meetings are packed with energy, emotionally charged, often like living theater or vaudeville. A teenage junkie does handsprings, parties are given, business is done, marriages are made. With all the actors, comedians and show business folks, the self-deprecating humor can be wicked and wonderful.

But how will I be able to go to AA dressed for Artie Gold's?

Well, if I go to the big meeting in Beverly Hills that Candice raved about, I'll be less conspicuous. Anyway, everyone is so naked emotionally that feelings usually overpower appearance.

Wearing a sexy party dress to a meeting will be a test. I have developed the habit of looking like a bag lady so that I won't have to deal with male egos making passes. Now, since I am a success, I have a responsibility to look like one. Then I think I would have that responsibility even if I were not a star. Looking good sets an example for newcomers.

Nevertheless, Friday night I struggle to put on my makeup. I sit at my vanity and think, Back to the drawing board. Candy, my silver tabby, perches on the window ledge watching me put on my eyeliner. Her amber-green eyes lined in black are more beautiful than any tabby's I've ever seen. As though she hears my thoughts, she turns her furry head and looks outside at an enormous pigeon flying by.

What would Scarlett wear? I select my sexiest cocktail dress, the one with the most frills. All velvet and lace, with thin shoulder straps and deep décolletage. Two black-net crinolines and one made of red organdy line the skirt, which falls just above the knee. After I spray myself with a generous amount of perfume, I look in the mirror and think, Not bad for thirty-four.

I tie my black satin sandals with three-inch heels, gather my belongings and am out the door, minutes later driving over Laurel Canyon wailing reggae along with Bob Marley. "Don't give up the fight! Get up! Stand up! Stand up for your rights!"

Parking is a problem. Cars are lined up along Rodeo Drive. Camden Drive. I park in a lot behind La Scala.

Walking up the stairs of the church rectory, I hear loud, hearty singing. "Happy Birthday to . . ." A piano plays. Three hundred people are celebrating another alcoholic's birthday. A candle representing one year of sobriety is placed on a home-made birthday cake.

I feel warmth. Joy. French alcoholics never sang.

• • •

The birthday girl says, "Hi, I'm Jane, an alcoholic/schizo-phrenic. And so am I." Everyone laughs. She doesn't feel sorry for herself. She doesn't want my pity. In fact I get the feeling it would piss her off tremendously.

I creep into a seat in the back of the room and feel people looking at me. They turn away. Most of them know I am a stranger to this group. A few men leer. I wish I had brought a shawl to wrap around my shoulders and hide my neckline.

I look around the room. All types. All ages. Black hair, brown hair, white, red and blue hair. Women in ponytails, men in ponytails. Mexicans, Chinese, Puerto Ricans, blacks, Japanese, WASPs, Jews, American Indians. Conservative dressers, leather queens, sex kittens, jeans, a few men in black tie and ladies in gowns. Are they going to Artie Gold's too, I wonder. Hetero-sexuals. Homosexuals. Bisexuals. Jesus freaks. Atheists. A tall woman with buckteeth clutches a large doll with gold curls. An astronaut sits beside her. I spot a talk-show host. A famous co-median. Last year's Oscar winner for best actor.

There's Joan—— (last names are rarely used), who wrote that best-seller about Washington. And Peter——, the comedian who jumped off the top of a hotel in Hollywood. Nancy——, the gorgeous actress who drove off a cliff and had to have her face reconstructed. Ellen——, who has been married eleven times, another addiction. Bill——, the actor from the '60s who admits to having been one of the first to use cocaine when he was acting in a movie. Jerry——, a top fashion photographer. Henry——, a composer. John——, the rock 'n' roller who killed his wife in a car crash on the Pacific Coast Highway. Perry——, who runs one of the best PR firms. Clive——, a black basketball player who just signed a million-dollar contract. Allen——, the owner of Carte Blanche Liquors. Oh, dear!

The bright neon shows everything: in this room there's no pretending. Wrinkles, crinkles, scars, tucks, makeup, yellowed whites of eyes—meaning a bad liver, usually belonging to a newcomer. There are few secrets. And those remaining are hard to hold on to.

At the break some of the stars mingle. A few keep to themselves. I want to talk to those I recognize, but don't feel a meeting is about social climbing. Then I think, Don't be silly, you could say hello. But it is still difficult for me to introduce myself to anyone.

I remain in my seat. So do the senior citizens on either side of me. Under the harsh light I notice a wrinkle in my cleavage. Suddenly I feel the woman on my left looking at me, then at my breasts. So is the woman on my right. They remind me of my mother. I want to flee. I grab my clutch bag and hold it over my chest and find a vacant seat in the front of the room.

I am so uptight. Because of the way I am dressed, because of the scandal about my flashing, because I am now being called a star. Feelings of success are so foreign to me.

The coffee break is almost over. All the watermelon, cheese, grapes, cookies, cakes and crackers have been eaten, and the coffee urns are empty.

The next speaker, Bob, a tall, robust Texan, has been in solitary confinement and now is a member of the most exclusive country club. He used to go through women's handbags at parties. He candidly tells about his stealing, a former addiction. Today he counsels alcoholics.

The third speaker, Sue Ann, appears to be in her early thirties, though she says she is forty-one. Her dark hair is severely slicked back off her face into a chignon. Her eyes are bright blue, brows thick, and her nose is sturdy and uneven—unusual for Hollywood. Her lips are delicate and thin and only reveal their sensuality when she says words with an "o" in them. At first glance she has the primness of a spinster schoolteacher, but when she laughs a glint in her eyes radiates a wild sensuality and her raucous laughter shows total abandonment. It makes you wonder what she was like when she drank.

"Hi, I'm Sue Ann, a grateful recovering alcoholic and star-fucker." People laugh. Some frown. Some whistle. "My story is—I slept with Hollywood." After the laughter subsides, the room becomes quiet, still. "After a few drinks, a low-neck dress and a few dirty words, I was in the bedroom. I didn't know how to talk to men. Wine did that for me." (Sue Ann was telling my story!) "My mother is a Quaker and raised me to believe sex was a sin. Pills and alcohol made me forget. During an orgasm I didn't hear my mother's nagging and didn't feel I was wrong... the only time I felt good about myself." No one moves. A doctor's beeper sounds, then is silenced.

"Eventually all the stars left me, and I ended up supporting a bisexual rock 'n' roll clothing designer with no teeth who I thought I couldn't live without." People laugh, identifying with Sue Ann's inability to be alone. "I even bought him new teeth. He preferred his stubs. After I was three years sober, I sold the story of my affairs with the stars to a newspaper and a book publisher on London's Fleet Street and was crowned the Queen of Kiss and Tell. I don't believe in secrets, or, as our Big Book says, closing the doors on our past." (The Big Book is AAs bible.) "I feel both women and men must take responsibility for what they've done and where they've been. Today I know I'm a pretty decent person—even nice on some days—and I would like to think those stars I've credited would be grateful to have had my privilege." Some men snicker. Sue Ann smiles an I-don't-give-a-damn smile. "I rejected more than I submitted to. Life's short. My regrets to them." A drunk yells, "You're full of shit!" Sue Ann says, "Probably." The drunk is removed during the laughter. "Some stars want to be in my book, and all men want to know what other men—especially stars—are like in bed, and so I made a great deal of money. This meant that I could afford to return to the university and become a sex therapist for women who like myself have spent most of their lives trying to please men and get the approval of the 'If you don't do what I tell you, I won't love you' type of man that I was obsessed with. Today I am free from that bondage."

People applaud. Some cheer, whistle. Some men leave. A few walked out during her story. Sex is a delicate topic at these meetings. People can talk about violence, death, murder, disease, suicide, rape, theft, incest, but plain old sexual intercourse of a heterosexual nature is most often frowned upon. The gay meetings are more open. Homosexuals know they have to talk about sexual guilt to be free of it.

I will get Sue Ann's number one day. I need someone with courage to replace Candice.

The longer I am in the meeting, the less I worry about the party. Though I don't share with anyone what I'm feeling, I too feel unburdened, and when the meeting is over I am eager to go to Artie Gold's soirée.

Slowly, feeling like my soul has been in a sauna, I walk to the parking lot, where Z and her driver are waiting.

ARTIE Gold's Bel Air mansion sparkles in the night. Klieg lights installed on a lawn the size of a golf course announce the party to the stratosphere. As we turn off Sunset Boulevard onto Bellagio Drive in Z's chauffeur-driven Bentley, we are forced to wait in a line along with some twenty other vehicles —limousines, sports cars, station wagons and jeeps, Hollywood's trendiest mode of transportation. To his exclusive "A list" party Artie is able to invite only five hundred. His fifty-room mansion, complete with Olympic-size swimming pool, Jacuzzi, game room, screening room, collection of Old Masters, tennis court, racquetball court, Nautilus equipment center, six caged chimpanzees and seventeen strolling peacocks, can hold no more. Artie Gold is a busy man. Before he made his millions he was a hardware salesman from the Bronx.

Z's Bentley finally arrives at the mansion's guardhouse. An attendant in a red Philip Morris–man uniform, holding a clipboard with a Xeroxed guest list, recognizes me.

"Mith Endicott," he says, "forgive me, but may I have your autograph?"

I smile and oblige, holding my cape tightly over my dress.

Our chauffeur pulls in front of the mansion. A valet opens the car door. Flashbulbs blind. Thrown off guard, I accidentally release my green velvet cape. Click! Click! Click! Chaos accomplishes modestly what I would have had to do immodestly. I laugh into the cameras.

"Maya, it's Gary," one photographer shouts, trying to get my attention for a head-on photo.

I smile in his direction. Gary who? Be kind to the press, I tell myself. They're doing a job too. Meanwhile I wonder if Mr. Gold publicizes his films as much as he publicizes his parties.

A butler wearing white gloves and no smile gives Z's ermine jacket and my cape to a maid, who gives us two plastic disks with numbers on them. Necks crane my way. I think of Tutu. I think of Candice. The crowd's attention feels good. I remember how I used to tremble when a group of people, especially strangers, looked at me. How I would avoid their gaze, feel disconnected. Tonight I look back at the throng, feeling eager to mingle. A part of the party. I inhale, pull down the bodice of my gown, raise my chin, turn to Z, who is decked out in silver sequins, and say, "Shall we?"

"Follow me, Scarlettina. Ain't it grand Sacha and Eric are out of town? Two gorgeous 'chick-lets' on the prowl. What could be more *gemütlich?*"

We descend three steps into the sunken living room. A mirrored baby grand, blue velvet sofas and dark antiques decorate the room. What appears to be a Turner hangs above a fireplace. The smell of burning logs mingles with the clash of perfumes, colognes and after-shaves. The massive chandelier could have just arrived from Vienna's Schoenbrun Palace. A large spiral staircase carpeted in royal green wall-to-wall dominates the main room. Where it leads—most eager starlets know.

The party is peaking. Z and I are two hours late. Hollywood etiquette. We survey the crowd. Z frowns as she adjusts her opal earrings. "They're all here tonight, Ms. Highbrow. Feel them plotting?" She looks at me sidewise and nudges my elbow. "Look, there's Merri Lee with Rob Delaney. That's some match!"

A trendy couple, both with short-cropped hair slicked down with pomade, lean against the mirrored baby grand and caress each other's thin, intravenously fed bodies.

"Doesn't she know he's gay?" I say in a whisper, looking down at the Oriental carpet.

"You mean doesn't he know she's gay?" says Z indifferently as she reaches into her purse and pulls out a turquoise cigarette. "C'mon, Ms. Hetero. Don't you think we're all basically bi-bi?"

A tuxedoed waiter offers us glasses of champagne or Perrier served on a glittering silver platter. Z takes the champagne and after a few sips licks her lips. "Ah, Dom Pérignon. Love that Artie and his gold."

I take a Perrier.

The waiter, who looks like he just got off lifeguard duty in Santa Monica, smiles as though he knows me. But of course. He sat in front of me at the meeting.

A guest pushes Z, who spills some of her champagne. "How can you tolerate these shindigs without drinking?"

"Tolerate?" I say, watching the waiter walk away. "This is fun."

Someone shouts from behind us, "Hey, Maya, what a film. Congrats! You outdid yourself." A beaming Marvin Winter slaps me on the back so that my cleavage jiggles and catches the eye of Stanley Meyer of Meyer, Kohn and Kubernick, a PR firm on the rise—just like the adrenaline of an eye-bulging Stanley.

"Thanks, Marvin," I say as Stanley grabs my left hand and squeezes it without any apparent intention of letting go.

"Maya, may I shake your hand," Stanley says, placing his back in Marvin's face and his eyes on my breasts, to which he continues to talk. "Your performance released a lot of repressed sexuality in my wife. Can't tell you how our sex life changed after seeing your film. Unfortunately, I feel it's better for both of us, the divorce. Oh, did I give you my new office number?" Stanley reaches in his wallet, pulls out a card and rubs his thumb over the engraved surface. "My private line is on the right." He smiles, clears his throat and for the first time looks into my eyes. Not a blink in sight.

Z grabs my elbow, saying, "We have to pee, Stan." I laugh and the Perrier I am about to swallow bursts out of my mouth onto Stanley's red face.

"Oh, Stanley, so sorry," I say, drying his face with my cocktail napkin. "More upset about your divorce. Excuse us before my friend has an accident on your brand-new patent leathers."

A disgruntled Z leads me through the horde of gawking merrymakers into the lounge—the size of my kitchen—adjacent to a bathroom. The door to the loo is locked. "Lordy, he's the worst! Smell his breath? June Anthony told me because of all his screwing around his wife stopped giving him rim jobs. Now he's divorcing her."

"Ever do that to Eric?"

"Stopped on our wedding night. He still does me."

I laugh. "How do you train men?"

"Grab 'em by the scrotum! How many times do I have to tell you, Ms. Magdalen? Read Harold Robbins!"

The door at the loo opens. A drunken bleached blonde with her nipples partially hanging over the top of her strapless gown stumbles by us. "Ooh, your conversation just grosses me out."

"Go back to the valley, girl. It's a lot cleaner than the shit that comes out of your mouth," Z says, flouncing into the toilet as Miss Valley Girl sits at a vanity table humming a jazzed-up version of "The Star-Spangled Banner" while she chews, blows and pops green bubbles and teases her already tangled hair.

I scrounge around in my handbag for a compact as an elegant brunette dressed in a black satin pantsuit enters, holding the elbow of a nervous redhead reeking of Giorgio, Beverly Hills' own perfume, the scent of money. They are oblivious to everyone.

"It was like an eraser! I swear it! Short and stubby," says the brunette in a gravelly voice with a cultivated-in-Burbank English accent.

"Not Phillip?"

"Yes, our darling local James Bond . . . I was expecting something possibly the size of my vibrator. At least with the enthusiasm."

"What a drag! He made you do all the work."

"Listen, Louisa, I'm used to it. In this town if you find cock that's hetero, be grateful!"

"Oh, Agnes, how right you are." Louisa bends over, throwing her big breasts into her push-up bra, then stands, pulling down the bodice of her sequined lavender stretch jumpsuit. "Maybe you should try Ralph."

"Ralph?"

"The cashier at Safeway. He makes these industry boys look like Little Lord Fauntleroys."

"Never tried Safeway," Agnes says, combing her pageboy.

"Monday, Wednesday, Friday. The express line." Louisa sticks her finger in a pot of fuchsia lip gloss.

Agnes stops combing and sticks her finger in Louisa's gloss. "Did I ever tell you about the guy whose testicles smelled? I had to take a 'lude to finish him off." Agnes smacks the gloss between her lips.

Miss Valley Girl belches, stands up and shouts, "Gross! Gross! Gross! You're a bunch of sickos!" She hiccups. "Let me outta here."

"Pleasure's mine," Agnes says, sitting at the vanity.

"What's her problem?" Louisa asks.

"The valley," Agnes says, flossing her front teeth.

"I just moved there," I say, smiling.

Louisa and Agnes, who have had their backs to me, turn to see who could live in the valley and admit it. Agnes spills powder on her pantsuit as her frown turns to a crooked grin. "Oscar time there, Ms. Endicott."

Louisa, who has been adding more mascara to her false

lashes, accidentally puts some on the tip of her nose. "I don't know how to say this," she says, rubbing her nostril. "I read about your ordeal. Thanks for your honesty and..." She hesitates, her nose bright red. She is on the verge of tears. "What I mean is... I've done stuff like that. I thought I was the only... Oh, it's so embarrassing." Louisa's tears loosen her individual lashes and one by one they fall onto her cheeks. "I need another drink," she says, blowing her nose.

Agnes puts her arm around Louisa. "I used to be into garage mechanics myself."

"Speaking of cock," Z says, storming out of the lounge as a fat, bald man chokes on his cigar smoke.

Grabbing my hand, Z leads me through the living room onto the patio, which is covered by a huge white tent.

Round Abbey-Rents tables decorated with bouquets of baby's breath and cymbidium, ivory candles and white tablecloths spread over the lawn. A buffet sits off to one side under a gigantic weeping willow. A portable dance floor placed over the swimming pool rises from the center of the lawn and somehow reminds me of an altar. A DJ wearing a Hawaiian shirt, sneakers and pink sunglasses stands by complex stereo equipment and injects cassettes. Out of the many speakers Frank Sinatra croons "My Way." Off in the distant bushes, the Valley Girl is throwing up.

Z and I stand on the patio and look out on the black-tied, taffetaed, and blue-jeaned crowd. In Hollywood it is chic to dress down.

The air is warm for mid-March. Santa Ana winds blow dry air in from the desert. Will the Santa Anas drive anyone crazy tonight, I wonder.

Plates clatter. Waiters scurry. The heady aroma of a mesquite grill—what the French call a *feu de bois*—reminds me of France. I miss Jean-Paul and Candice.

My eyes scan the multitude, trying to spot AA's I had seen at the meeting. Friendly heads turn. Some too-friendly heads turn.

Z and I begin our party stroll, nodding to the few unseated, unfamished, overly thirsty stragglers while moving on to a secluded corner of the long, white, wrought-iron bar.

Z and I place our purses on the bar and watch the jam-packed dance floor. Above the dancers a large mirrored ball rotates, flashing blue, pink and purple rays of light down onto closely pressed bodies.

Z's eyes widen. Her heavily mascaraed lashes touch her thick brows. "Look at slimy Herbie Saks grabbing Darian Nelson away from that wimp George Wannaker."

Squinting, I see a big, full-breasted blonde pressed against a greasy, pock-faced, gangsterlike type. "Why's she dancing with him?"

"'Cause he's clutching her like an orangutan, that's why. Besides, Ms. Straight Arrow, she's an old pussy-bumper from way back. Doesn't give a cootie about men."

I nearly choke on my maraschino cherry. "Darian's gay?"

Z nods, raises a brow and places a black-gloved palm on her silver-sequined hip. "Open your pupes, Ms. Naïveté. He's drunk!"

"She's drunk," I say, digging in my handbag for my glasses, slipping the gold-rims over my nose. "What a great jumpsuit."

"Paper. Edible. Only eighteen beans." Z finishes her champagne and signals the bartender for a refill. "Can't wear underwear . . . shows through the white."

The bartender, who looks like a moonlighting bodybuilder, ignores Z to watch Darian.

Suddenly the music changes from the crooning of Frank Sinatra to the screaming of the O'Jays oldie but goodie "Backstabbers." The DJ turns up the volume.

I bite into a freshly manicured cuticle. "Dracula's dragging her around like she's Raggedy Ann. Let's rescue her, Z."

Z sighs, tapping the wrought iron with her empty glass. "Thought you were out of the hospital, Ms. Puritan Ethics?"

The muscle-bound bartender a few feet away signals to Z, "In a minute." Then he spreads his arms over the bar and leans forward. As he stares at a frenzied, bedroom-haired Darian, whose breasts—the only part of her body not being groped—flail in time with the music, Mr. Muscle-bound grinds his teeth while his black bow tie bounces up and down each time he swallows. Which is often.

The thirty tables are now crammed with at least ten guests, more interested in the brightly lit dance floor than small talk, while the other dancing couples have moved aside to watch.

A leering, drooling, coked-up Herbie, head jerking up and down, stomps confidently yet peculiarly out of time with the music while Darian grimaces, desperately clutching his black leather jacket and gold chains.

"Her jumpsuit's going to rip!" I say.

"Since when do you care about Darian? Oops!" Z makes a clucking sound with her tongue. "It just did! In the crotch!"

The bartender lets out a *wha-hoo!* as though a home run's been hit, slaps his fist into a palm the size of Shea Stadium and grins, showing every perfect molar.

I make a meal of my lower lip. "Poor Darian. Why, she's a brunette! Poor thing hasn't the foggiest idea this has happened."

An angry, dehydrated Z grabs a bottle of champagne already open. "She'll know fast enough. She'll feel a draft or get propositioned by that leering Wes Bromfman. It wouldn't be the first time he's gone down in public."

The guests are enjoying the humiliating spectacle. My enjoyment has ended. "We can't just stand here gaping, Z."

"What're you gonna do? Lend her your panties?" Z does a Gypsy Rose Lee with a black satin glove, slowly pulling it off and dangling it in front of my nose. "You may have stopped drinking, Ms. Hypocrite, but I doubt if you've started wearing underwear." (Z knew me inside and out.) "Besides, I thought you hated her."

I raise my chin and put on my best smiling imitation of Bozo. "That was the past. Let's get some food. Give me a rundown on what's been happening while I've been in ungay Paree."

The O'Jays have stopped screaming. The DJ takes a break. The sounds of laughter and buzz of gossip become the new but oh-so-familiar soundtrack.

A guilty-looking Mr. Muscle-bound lumbers over to Z. "Champagne?" He recognizes me. "Oh, Ms. Endicott, may I have your autograph?"

Z raises her arm like a traffic cop. "Had your chance, Muscle Beach. Next time try developing something besides pecs and erections." Z grabs my elbow as we walk over to the buffet. "Keep moving. Here come more fans, Ms. Hot Box Office."

We weave through the guests, partake of the caterer's efforts and sit under a tall oak tree at a table being cleared by a sun-tanned, surf-loving waiter.

"I like to watch," I say, spreading my caviar as I take in the surroundings.

"So the delivery boy said," Z says, pulling a leg off her Cornish hen.

My caviar looks less appetizing. "Careful. Not too secure about that. Yet."

Z nibbles at the chicken leg. "Better accept it, girl, 'cause all of H'wood has. You're hot gossip, Ms. Oscar Contender." Z sucks each finger clean like Italian nobility at a porno, then leans back and looks at the table behind me. "Oh, there's Sue Ann Pennypacker!"

I recognize her from the meeting. "Is she still writing about the stars?"

"Yep, same tune." Z spreads a thick slice of pâté onto French bread.

"Doesn't she worry about being sued?" I say, looking over my shoulder, feigning interest in one of the seventeen strolling pea-cocks behind Sue Ann, who is dressed in a dark, tailored suit and a white silk shirt.

Z bites into her pâté. "Sue Ann's as honest as Saint Joan. More boring, but as honest." A chunk of pâté falls into her cleavage. While digging for it she says, "Let those star-studded pen-i take her to court! Humph!" Z puts the crumbs into her mouth and with her napkin rubs her pâté-smeared breasts, which bounce as she speaks. "I can just see it. Judge asks her to describe the attributes and imperfections of the plaintiff's prized possession—erect or vacationing." Z now imitates Sue Ann. "'Why, Your Honor, he has a tattoo saying "Mother" under his left testicle.' Whereupon the plaintiff is taken behind closed doors. Examined by a horny proctologist. The star loses, then turns around and sues the proctologist."

"Z, you should write a book."

"I'd rather brag aloud."

At the next table I notice a tall, dapper, gray-haired gentleman towering over novelist June Anthony. "Who's the handsome old geezer asking June to dance?"

"Literary agent—Manny 'Self-Righteous' Weiss," Z says with a sneer. "H'wood's head host. Note *le double entendre*. Ya don't need him anymore, Ms. Lily White. He pimps for stars, studio heads, writers. That's how his properties get made into movies. Eighty-five."

"So spry!"

"When you've seen what he has, it's bound to keep you on your toes." Z looks behind herself, signaling a passing waiter for another glass of champagne. "There's that gorgeous Dan Tapplinger cruising with that woman-hater Claude Ainsworthy. Ekk!" She shoves a toothpick into her mouth, then pulls it slowly from between her thick lips. "Dan's the best I ever had. I had my period. He said, 'So what?' and went down on me anyway! He's gonna be a big star!"

I spill Perrier on my lap and smile.

From several feet away Dan Tapplinger and beady-eyed Claude Ainsworthy look at me. They approach our table.

Z pulls out her gold compact and studies herself in the mirror.

"Ever made it with Claude?" I say, wiping off the Perrier.

"Bluebeard? Sure. Have to if you want to be in his films. He once gave a dinner party and for dessert hanged his poodle over the table."

I feel like vomiting. "I don't believe it."

"I was there. He's scum. Pure scum. One night I sat on his pearlike, bulbous stomach and kept trying to come when he looks up from behind his cootie-ridden beard and yells, 'What's wrong with you? Can't you relax?' Glad I had Ecstasy to pop! Imagine how it feels to be directed by him?"

Claude and Dan, now a few feet away, are smiling like they will tell my mother my deepest secret unless I do what they want me to do. I guess they don't know I don't believe in secrets.

A gloating Claude with red veins making a road map out of his face is about to introduce himself. He recognizes Z and nudges Dan, who looks at his watch as they quickly turn away.

Z's eyes swell. She opens her purse, pulls out a Valium and washes it down with champagne.

"Z, you're doing a Karen Quinlan. That combination will kill you!"

"He sodomized me on my kitchen table and can't even say hello. Improve yourself, Ms. Holier-Than-Thou, instead of trying to fix me. Isn't that what's under all that mania to rescue people? You keep seeing what's wrong with others. Why don't you see what's wrong with you?"

"Sorry, Z. Thanks." I put my hand on her wrist. She pulls away and lights another cigarette. The wrong end.

"Damn!" she says when she sees the filter tip flame.

I think, Change the subject. Two tables away sits an enormous chunk of Cro-Magnon male flesh. "There's Yugoslavia's James Bond!"

Z inhales and angrily blows smoke rings in the direction of our man.

"I remember when I was so wrapped up in getting men to want me," I say.

"You still are," Z says, flicking ashes on the Astroturf. "All you talk about is Sacha, Sacha, Sacha."

"Hey, Z, it's getting better."

"Send me a postcard," she says, blowing smoke Dragon Lady–like out of her nostrils while tapping the table with her crimson nails.

"Anyway, one night I was so drunk Yugoslavia refused to do it to me. So, naked, I stood on my head. Did a split and sang, 'I wanna be loved by you, jus' you . . . boo-boo-be-do.' He liked my singing. Don't underestimate the splendor of the Dalmatian coast. What I remember of it, anyway."

Z stops drumming on the table and grins. "Ever had Tony di Angelo?"

"When did you sneak him in?"

"When you was in Paree." Z's eyes soften. Her lips move slowly. Her words slur.

"Report!"

"Tattoos all over! Great body, but monosyllabic. Leaves his socks on," Z says, yawning. "He looks to fuck starlets who won't talk."

"Why doesn't he go to a morgue? Oh, there's Rolf Bismarck," I say in a German accent, staring at a lean, dark-eyed man with finely chiseled features wearing a top hat and tails and carrying a walking stick. "Now there's a star who gives good dialogue. Lousy head. In fact, no head. Plays with himself. Swiss," I say, yawning, mimicking Z.

"What's this schmaltz? 'Arrivederci, Roma'?" Z sits up and glares at the DJ, then smiles. "Claudio Montenegro's in from Positano. That's why they're playing this dreck. One night he comes home for coffee." Z clears her throat. "I excuse myself for the loo and am sittin' there when you-know-who barges in with an erection the size of that tower in Pisa and shoves it in my mouth. Blow job Italian style. I didn't complain."

We both sit there with our cheeks between our fists watching Claudio as he moves around the dance floor.

Suddenly a hand taps my shoulder. A hairy wrist connected to a palm the size of Yankee Stadium holds a piece of torn notebook paper. I look up into the face of Mr. Muscle-bound.

"Hey, Ms. Endicott, please. My kid brother's handicapped. Name's Jake, and you know . . . sorry about ignoring you both at the bar. Darian's an ex. She pulled some rotten stuff." Brown eyes look sincerely out from under big, thick lids. Everything about him is big and thick.

"Of course," I say. "What's your name?"

"Tom. Tom Bishop."

Z cocks her head to one side and says with a slur, "I'm Zoe. Friends call me Z." She extends her gloved hand. "Wanna dance, Tom?"

"One dance, sure. I need the exercise."

"I'll give you some," Z says, leaning over as she presses her palms on the table and her elbows against her breasts. Slowly she stands up.

Tom stares at her alabaster spa-pampered skin.

I scribble my name on the wrinkled piece of paper and hand it to him.

Z shakes her shoulders. Sequins shimmer.

Tom looks like he is about to regress to breast-feeding days.

"That's Bo Diddley they're playing," Z says with a squeal.

Her lithe body drenched in sequins slithers off to the center of the dance floor, then glistens under the spotlights. Her dancing is down and dirty.

I lean back in my chair and watch the candlelight flicker on the baby's breath. A peacock passes by. I offer it a strawberry. It too walks away. I think of how I used to feel abandoned sitting alone at a party, but tonight I feel content. Happy to be quiet. To listen instead of talk. To look instead of listen.

Someone clears his throat and says, "Excuse me." A frail, white-haired, green-eyed Englishman wearing a diamond stick-pin in an amber ascot extends a graceful hand. "Allow me to introduce myself. Sherman Elliot. I want to say how thrilled Mr. Gold and I are at the possibility of your playing Scarlett O'Hara."

"Oh, how kind of you," I say, offering him a seat. I study his pale, sensitive face and wonder why such a distinguished man would work with such a sleazeball as Artie Gold. Sherman's eyes are impossible to read.

"Mr. Gold wants me to tell you he's so pleased you have come tonight, and he'll be over momentarily."

I get it. A trade-off. Artie's gold for Sherman's class and talent. I hear clanging. Bells ringing. Silver jangling. Saved by an approaching Z. Sherman leaves the moment she introduces herself. "Some hunky number," she says, mopping perspiration from her neck and brow.

"Sherman?"

"Heavens, no! Muscle Beach!"

"So where is he?"

"Tending. Rendezvous at midnight."

"What's Elliot's story?"

"Gold's pimp."

"Figures."

"Still one of the best directors in the biz."

"I should have worn my chastity belt."

"Just your chastity mouth. Get the part. Practice tolerance, compassion, like you're supposed to, Sister Carrie."

"Speaking of directors, there go the Clark brothers. Remember when Wally couldn't get hired? I had affairs with both of them at the same time, separately. Don't think they knew. One day Randy calls minutes before Wally calls on my other line. I put Randy on hold. Then Wally. It's fun directing directors. Felt like an orgy with Pacific Telephone." I laugh, remembering how I liked to control men, then wondered why they left me.

"Which was better?" Z says, freshening her makeup.

"Even though he has one ball, Wally's hung better. Lasts

longer but Randy's more kinky. Better mind. I'll take the mind
any day."

"Not without the rest, I hope. I wouldn't want to lose you to
the Beverly Hills library." Z scans the crowd for another dancing partner.

"I bottomed out on libraries in Paris. Thank you very much
indeed."

"Ever make it with a guy, some cheap wine and a quart of
chocolate ice cream?"

"Z, you're certifiable."

"Seeing Ernie Gross dancing just now reminded me of the
night in Room 210 of the Beverly Wilshire. Why don't these
guys say hello? You'd think a friendly boff would bring ladies
and gents closer. In this town intercourse creates enemies."

"Do you say hello to Ernie?"

"Well, I think he should say hello to me first. Anyway, Eric's
jealous of my matinees." Z stares at what must be her sixth glass
of champagne, then says sharply, "What are you—a watch cat?
Right! I don't say hello to them, Ms. Holmes." Z kicks the table
leg.

Change the subject, I tell myself. "Ever tell you about the
time with Biff Morgan when we did a lot of grass, and he looked
up from between my legs and asked, 'Where are ya?' I didn't
have the heart to tell him a sale at Macy's. It was six o'clock.
The store was closing. I couldn't decide between a turquoise bra
and a yellow one. Never used that weed again."

"Hey, the Crusades ended in 1066 A.D., Wilhelmina the Con-
queror. Look at Swen Johanson falling all over June. He wants
to be in her book, I'll bet. He's some tennis player. Better lover.
Came three times in two hours. Has this kinky, fat masseur,
looks like Mr. Clean. Fattie watched his boss work me out in the
bedroom while peeping through the open door. Next morning
Swen went off to a match, and Mr. Clean gave me a massage.
Ripped my jeans in the crotch. I needed a vacation after that
lot."

"Always thought tennis players were spoiled little boys," I

say, nibbling on a strawberry dipped in chocolate.

"We were talking about screwing, Ms. Freud. Not psychoanalyzing. Just because I like to fuck someone doesn't mean I like them."

"What would men do if they knew we talked like this?"

"How do you think they talk about us, Ms. Clorox Breath?"

"I wonder." I shove the strawberry in the dirty ashtray.

"If you think that's crass, hey, deodorant isn't used in the men's locker room only for body odor. Locker-room mouth makes me look as virtuous as Ms. Melanie, Ms. Scarlett."

Z drums her fingers on the table. "Oh, there's Artie Gold. Give the old coot five minutes. Whaddaya got to lose?"

"Not my virginity." I squint, too vain to put on my glasses. "Not bad for a producer."

"Surfaces. Schmerfaces. Creep has everything moola can buy. 'Cept women. Keeps Xeroxed lists of 'Starlets Wanted' in his glove compartment, by his vitamins, under his VCR and above the toilet paper dispenser in his bathroom. After he fucks a target, she's crossed off La List. Bedroom's bugged with heavy-duty zoom lens video cameras. He's heard about your aberrant behavior, Ms. Flash, and is turned on to broil. Get that part. Your chance to redeem yourself, Scarlett. Tomorrow's tonight."

A slim pocked-faced Artie with faint traces of scabs from a recent hair transplant says hello to Z, then extends a trim, hairy hand bearing a gold ring with a crest.

"Hello, Mr. Gold," I say, looking into enlarged pupils staring out from under puffy Quaalude eyelids.

Artie smiles and out of the corner of his mouth says in a raspy voice, "Don't be so formal, Maya."

I stare into the yellowed whites of his eyes and count the red veins, thinking, Let this creep do the talking if he's going to put me down.

Z senses my feelings. "Artie, be gentle with Maya. She's had a rough time."

"I heard all about it," he says, continuing to glare at me.

"I can take care of myself, Ms. Z," I say in as seductive a southern accent as I can muster.

I feel his magnetism. His power to denigrate still appeals to some sick part of me. I notice his parched lips lined in a white film—traces of cocaine, fear. Power games. More fear. He pulls a small bottle out of his pocket and rubs it in my hand. "Come with me. I want to see how you feel about starring in GWTW, the sequel. Excuse us, Z," he says without so much as a glance in her direction.

I trudge along by his side, wondering why. Over the patio, through the living room, up the spiral staircase. Feeling like Big Red Riding Hood. We pass his bedroom, decorated in baby blue and white with a king-sized bed covered by a comforter and a canopy trimmed in eyelet. Artie hasn't been weaned from Mama.

A line of frustrated dopers and sexually aroused newly-mets mingle with those who have a genuine need to use the bathroom. Artie takes my hand and walks to the front of the line while joking with his guests. The door opens. An older man quickly exits. A young girl tearfully follows, trying to wipe a white stain out of her black dress.

Artie leads me into his master bath. Mirrors cover the walls, the floor, the ceiling. By a marble bidet a green candle flickers the fragrance of jasmine. The circular travertine bathtub-cum-Jacuzzi is bigger than the kiddies' pool at Allentown, Pa.'s swim club. Three steps lead to a thronelike mahogany chair with a wicker seat which lifts, revealing a toilet. The chair's wooden armrests curve into enormous golden claws designed to hold on to. Could millionaire Gold, who seems to have everything, have a problem with constipation? A photo of Marilyn Monroe in an ornate silver frame hangs above a gilded toilet paper dispenser. That list Z spoke about must be hidden behind Marilyn's smiling face.

"Don't mind if I take the best seat in the house?" I say, sitting on the wooden throne.

"My face is the best seat in the house, my dear," Artie says, washing his hands as though preparing for surgery.

"Is that a statement or part of the deal?" I feign a yawn, not wanting to react to his manipulation. Why am I here? Something about old Artie still appeals to me. His power. False as it is. His desire to control me. To ultimately degrade me. It makes me want to play with him. Challenge him. Degrade *him*. If he were only a cabbie, a delivery boy, a gas station attendant, I could let myself go. Do it to him. But he is a Hollywood producer. One of those corporate kings who get off on exploiting women. Game time. I feel that buzz. That hum.

Artie dries his hands on a black monogrammed towel, then stands in front of me, grabbing the throne's golden claws with each hand. I smell his strong cologne as he leans toward me and stares into my eyes. "It's a package deal and I come with it."

"Are we here to discuss business or sex?"

"Pleasing men is business."

I want to hit him. I feel hot. Tingling.

He leans closer. His breath smells of garlic, which his expensive cologne can't hide. "Any star who wants to do Scarlett will have to do me. In my sequel Scarlett becomes a lady of the night, hoping to run into Rhett in a brothel. There will be sex with strangers. Her sexual charms . . . outrageous lack of inhibitions . . . now an alcoholic . . . make her famous. Like your test for *The Starlet*. But film can lie. Lighting, camera angles . . . tricks. I must see your face sexually charged. In the flesh."

"People are waiting," I say, though I love the drama. Being where others want to be—even if it's only a bathroom—still appeals to me.

"Maya, I only have fifteen peepee parlors. If those assholes want to wait, let 'em." Artie stops clutching his golden claws and pulls out his coke vial and silver spoon. "A toke relaxes."

"No, thanks," I say, feeling that burning, not wanting to feel that throbbing. My addiction doesn't need a substance. His raspy voice talks to that repressed, dark part of me. I like his voice. Hate him. What he is trying to do to me. Yet I am turned on. Why after all these months is this still happening? The doctors say I need time. Time for demons with no self-worth to be exorcised. Self-deprecating monsters deep inside that now want to come out. Fuck it! I'm human. I'll stop when I'm ready. I feel like ripping off my dress.

"What if I don't want the part under your conditions?" I ask.

"Then you're a fool," Artie says, inhaling cocaine, which sticks to his nostrils. "Getting to know the emotional parameters of talent is my business. I never cast an actress who does not reveal herself emotionally. In an intimate . . . as the camera would see it . . . naked state."

What a dumb asshole. Ol' Artie needs a new line-writer. I'll play because I want to. Perspiration creeps out of my thighs. My skin sticks to the wicker seat. I throw my right leg over an armrest and say in a southern drawl, "I'll show you mine if you show me yours. I like to get to know my producers, too." A golden claw juts out from between my legs. I feel on fire.

"Why, I'd be delighted, Ms. Endicott," Artie says, then loosens his tie, locks the bathroom door and steps into his dressing room on the far side of the Jacuzzi.

Guests pound at the door. Someone shouts, "What are you doing? Counting the Charmin?"

The dressing room door opens and out walks a naked Artie proudly modeling an open trench coat and a protruding erection.

I can't laugh, though I want to. It's too sad. Too funny. It's me. I understand.

Still, he's one of them; the game must go on. "My, what a beautiful cock you have, Mr. Gold," I say, knowing this is what he wants to hear. "Shall we continue with the business at hand . . ."

Artie strokes himself gently, humming—excited at the thought that we will soon be exposing ourselves together.

My move. I take my time. This is going to be fun. I pull my

skirt up to the top of my thighs, not yet revealing myself. "I'll play your Scarlett for one million."

Artie yanks at himself and says, hissing, "Five hundred thousand."

I lift out my breasts. "A million five and I'm yours."

Artie spits saliva on himself. "You drive a hard bargain, Ms. Endicott."

"Not as hard as the cock you're holding," I say, caressing my nipples.

"Very funny, Maya."

"Getting a bit familiar, Mr. Gold? Ms. Endicott to you. This is business."

"Ms. Endicott, don't you feel your agent should handle this?" He pulls at himself in smooth steady strokes.

"Your cock?" I say, laughing. He wants abuse. Give it to him. It's part of the game. He's losing and doesn't even know it. "I conduct all my affairs, Mr. Gold," I say, throwing my left leg over the other gold claw.

A red-faced Artie stares at my blackness and jerks at his self-worth. "Well, go on, Ms. Endicott."

"When I'm ready," I say slowly.

About to come, he wants me to join him.

I can't touch myself. Something's happening. I feel cold. Frozen. Embarrassed.

Artie senses my feelings. "Your pussy hairs are shorter than on film."

"But your plugs look great!" I look down at the scabs on his forehead. At my body. At my legs spread in front of a man jerking off underneath a trench coat. I feel silly. Look silly. I *am* silly.

Suddenly I pull up my bodice, close my legs, walk to the door, turn back to an ecstatic Artie and say, "Sorry, Mr. Gold, but I have to be at Paramount in the morning." When I open the door, the incensed crowd composed of Sue Ann Pennypacker, Herbie Saks, Rolf Bismarck, Wes Bromfman, Stanley Meyer,

Darian Nelson, Ernie Gross, Marvin Winter, June Anthony, Louisa and Agnes, the Valley Girl and Gary the photographer push by just as a wailing Artie Gold—naked except for the trench coat, now at his knees—orgasms.

I raise my chin, walk by the gaping crowd and can't resist saying, "He likes my work."

As I pass through Artie's bedroom, I ask Z, cuddled in a corner with Muscle Beach, if her driver would take me to my car, still parked in Beverly Hills.

Twenty minutes later I am driving with the top down along a deserted Mulholland Drive in the moonlight, turning over the cassette and singing with Bob Marley, "We don't need no trouble. What we need is love. Sweet love!"

What a beautiful night!

I pull off the road. I take off my shoes and stockings, get out of the car and stand on the edge of a precipice high above the canyons and look down at the view, to watch the stars, to smell the honeysuckle, to hear the crickets, to feel the dirt between my bare toes. Along the horizon the sky is purple. The warm Santa Ana winds blow my hair from my face.

I think of Sacha. If it makes him happy, I hope he is raising skirts.

I think I'll raise mine. Why should Artie Gold have my last flash? Laughing, with legs spread I stand on the edge of an isolated cliff overlooking Hollywood, lift my skirt and all its crinolines high over my head, feel the warm air rushing up my thighs and make a fist, shoving it to the heavens. In the stillness of the night I shout to the stars, "I'm a grateful recovering alcoholic and exhibitionist. Yes, I am!" And I laugh. If I'm going to flash for the last time, why not flash all of Hollywood? I can't believe it. I think I'm beginning to enjoy life. Can this be true? Is it true? I know it's true. The warm air rushing up my thighs is the most wonderful warm air. I laugh again.